CLASSIC *f*M

ONE HUNDRED FAVOURITE HUMOROUS POEMS

CLASSIC *f*M
ONE HUNDRED FAVOURITE HUMOROUS POEMS

Introduction and biographies of the poets by
Mike Read

Hodder & Stoughton

First published in Great Britain in 1998 by Hodder and Stoughton
A division of Hodder Headline PLC

A Hodder & Stoughton paperback

19 18 17 16 15 14 13 12

A CIP catalogue record for this
title is available from the British Library.

ISBN 0 340 72833 7

Typeset by Palimpsest Book Production Limited,
Polmont, Stirlingshire
Printed and bound in Great Britain by
Mackays of Chatham PLC

Hodder and Stoughton
A division of Hodder Headline PLC
338 Euston Road
London
NW1 3BH

CLASSIC *f*M

ONE HUNDRED FAVOURITE HUMOROUS POEMS

Contents

vi

Introduction

While thinking about how to write a different introduction to a book of humorous poems, I began to amuse myself by thinking of the links between the poets featured in the Top One Hundred. I ended up with something that's almost a poem in itself, which might be called *Stanley Holloway in Thirty Moves*.

Stanley Holloway made his debut in *Kissing Time*, co-written with P. G. Wodehouse;

P. G. Wodehouse wrote with the Gershwins, whose song 'I Don't Think I'll Fall In Love Again' was influenced by G. K. Chesterton;

G. K. Chesterton was best friends with Hilaire Belloc;

Hilaire Belloc's book *The Four Men* influenced *The Soldier* by Rupert Brooke;

Rupert Brooke's early poems were published in *Granta* magazine, once edited by A. A. Milne;

A. A. Milne successfully adapted Kenneth Grahame's *The Wind In The Willows* for the stage, as did Alan Bennett;

Alan Bennett contributed to the book *Larkin at Sixty*, a celebration of Philip Larkin's life and work;

Philip Larkin was the librarian at Hull University where he met and influenced a young student called Roger McGough;

Roger McGough wrote hit records, as did Cole Porter;

Cole Porter wrote the music and lyrics for *Kiss Me Kate* based on the *Taming of the Shrew* by Shakespeare. The Shakesperian characters Othello, Richard III, Hamlet and Macbeth were all portrayed on stage by William McGonagall;

William McGonagall's American counterpart was Julia Moore (known as the American McGonagall) who was a major influence on Ogden Nash;

Ogden Nash wrote the musical *One Touch of Venus* with Kurt Weill, who wrote *Lady in the Dark* with Ira Gershwin, who wrote with P. G. Woodhouse;

P. G. Woodhouse was knighted, as was John Betjeman;

John Betjeman was at Marlborough School with Louis MacNeice;

Louis MacNeice described John Cornford as 'The first inspiring communist I have met': John Cornford was christened Rupert John Cornford in memory of Rupert Brooke;

Rupert Brooke was remembered in the poem *At Granchester* by Charles Causley;

Charles Causley wrote the poem at number 35 in the Top 100 called *Betjeman 1984*;

John Betjeman bought a new book of poems in 1976, and praised it as full of 'Good honest country poems': it was a collection by Pam Ayres;

Pam Ayres presented a radio documentary about Jane Austen who read and was influenced by William Cowper;

William Cowper's father was a rector, as was Lewis Carroll's;

Lewis Carroll's *The Hunting of the Snark* was influenced by *Bab Ballads* by W. S. Gilbert;

W. S. Gilbert almost became the artist for the *Alice* books by Lewis Carroll;

Lewis Carroll was educated at Rugby, as was Walter Savage Landor;

Walter Savage Landor was the model for Lawrence Boythorn in Dickens' *Bleak House*. The 1960s musical *Oliver*, based on Dickens' novel *Oliver Twist*, starred Barry Humphries;

Barry Humphries was a regular contributor to *Private Eye Magazine*, home of E. J. G. Thribb;

E. J. Thribb was created by Richard Ingrams – one of the founders of *Private Eye* magazine, while the founder of the Eton College magazine *The Etonian* was W. M. Praed;

W. M. Praed's work was often compared to that of Thomas Hood;

Thomas Hood was the joint editor of the *London Magazine*; The joint editor of the *Classical Review* was A. D. Godley;

A. D. Godley's translations of Horace were published in 1898, while another poet to translate Horace was Rupert Brooke;

Rupert Brooke's cousin Erica was infatuated with George Bernard Shaw, whose play *Pygmalion* became *My Fair Lady* and starred . . . Stanley Holloway!

So there you are! Thank you, Classic *f*M listeners, for voting for the *Top One Hundred Humorous Poems*, and giving me the opportunity to put this book together. I hope you enjoy it.

– Mike Read, August 1998

The Alto's Lament – Bob the Organist

When I first read this on Classic *f*M in 1997 I was completely unprepared for the deluge of letters asking for a copy. It really was an extraordinary response, which continued to flow steadily; the river burst its banks whenever it got another reading.

It flies the flag for the lady altos whose grievance that they are never allowed to star in any choral piece is poured into these five verses. Strangely, though, it appears to have been written by a man, who we only know as 'Bob' the organist, and was discovered behind the vestry door of All Saints Church, Four Oaks, Sutton Coldfield. Are you still out there, Bob? Or is that a pseudonym for a disgruntled West Midlands alto?

It's essential to find Bob or discover who he was, even if he's pulling out all the stops in that great organ loft in the sky. He deserves recognition. After all, he's beaten the likes of Carroll, Lear, Betjeman, Eliot, Belloc and Chesterton to the honour of being voted number one.

1

THE ALTO'S LAMENT

It's tough to be an alto when you're singing in the choir
The sopranos get the twiddly bits that people all admire,
The basses boom like loud trombones, the tenors shout
    with glee,
But the alto part is on two notes (or, if you're lucky, three).

And when we sing an anthem and we lift our hearts
    in praises
The men get all the juicy bits and telling little phrases.
Of course the trebles sing the tune – they always come
    off best;
The altos only get three notes and twenty-two bars rest.

We practise very hard each week from hymn-book and
    the Psalter,
But when the conductor looks at us our voices start
    to falter;
'Too high! Too low! Too fast! – you held that note
    too long!'
It doesn't matter what we do – it's certain to be wrong!

Oh! shed a tear for altos, they're the Martyrs and they
  know,
In the ranks of choral singers they're considered very low.
They are so very 'umble that a lot of folk forget 'em;
How they'd love to be sopranos, but their vocal chords
  won't let 'em!

And when the final trumpet sounds and we are wafted
  higher,
Sopranos, basses, tenors – they'll be in the Heavenly Choir.
While they sing 'Alleluia!' to celestial flats and sharps,
The altos will be occupied with polishing the harps.

EDWARD LEAR
1812–88

Lear was born on 12 May 1812, the twentieth child of a stockbroker who shortly afterwards went bankrupt. A sickly child, Lear suffered from epilepsy, asthma, bronchitis and, understandably, depression. However, he discovered that he had a talent for sketching flowers and birds and began to earn a living through his ornithological drawings. He was engaged by Lord Stanley, the 14th Earl of Derby, to draw the birds and animals in his menagerie, but Lear also started to write and illustrate nonsense poems to entertain the younger members of the Stanley family. In 1845 he published a collection of limericks, a form which he could not claim to have invented but which he certainly made his own. Accompanied by his companion Giorgio Cocali, he travelled extensively around the Mediterranean before settling in San Remo in 1870. He died in San Remo on 29 January 1888 and is buried there with Cocali and his beloved cat Foss.

The Owl and the Pussy-cat – Edward Lear

This all-time favourite nonsense poem of Edward Lear was first published in 1871, and appeared in *Nonsense Songs*, which also contained 'The Jumblies'. Charles Kingsley claimed that *Nonsense Songs* contained more wit and genius than Victorian philosophers like Herbert Spencer, who extended Darwin's Theory of Evolution, ever managed.

No one has ever been *quite* sure what a runcible spoon is, but it has been said that Lear's invention is a fork curved like a spoon, with three broad prongs, one of which has a sharp cutting edge.

It has been suggested that he based the word on *rouncival*, meaning a large pea. In Lear's *How Pleasant to Know Mr Lear*, however, there is mention of a runcible hat, so where does that leave us?

I'll leave you to think about the Bong-tree . . .

2

THE OWL AND THE PUSSY-CAT

I

The Owl and the Pussy-cat went to sea
  In a beautiful pea-green boat,
They took some honey, and plenty of money,
  Wrapped up in a five-pound note.
The Owl looked up to the stars above,
  And sang to a small guitar,
'O lovely Pussy! O Pussy, my love,
  What a beautiful Pussy you are,
    You are,
    You are!
  What a beautiful Pussy you are!'

II

Pussy said to the Owl, 'You elegant fowl!
  How charmingly sweet you sing!
O let us be married! too long we have tarried:
  But what shall we do for a ring?'
They sailed away, for a year and a day,
  To the land where the Bong-tree grows
And there in a wood a Piggy-wig stood
  With a ring at the end of his nose,
    His nose,
    His nose,
  With a ring at the end of his nose.

III

'Dear Pig, are you willing to sell for one shilling
   Your ring?' Said the Piggy, 'I will.'
So they took it away, and were married next day
   By the Turkey who lives on the hill.
They dined on mince, and slices of quince,
   Which they ate with a runcible spoon;
And hand in hand, on the edge of the sand,
   They danced by the light of the moon,
     The moon,
     The moon,
   They danced by the light of the moon.

LEWIS CARROLL
1832–98

Lewis Carroll was the pseudonym of Charles Dodgson, who was born at Daresbury near Warrington on 27 January 1832, the son of a clergyman. At the age of eleven he moved with his family to Croft in North Yorkshire. Carroll was educated at Rugby and at Christ Church, Oxford, and from an early age was fascinated by writing.

In 1855 Carroll took up a post as Lecturer in Mathematics at Christ Church, Oxford. On a picnic on the banks of the Thames with the daughters of the Dean, Dr Liddell, he began to spin the tale which was to turn into *Alice's Adventures in Wonderland*. Carroll used Alice Liddell, one of the daughters, as the model for the central character in the story. When published, with illustrations by Sir John Tenniel, the book became so popular that a sequel, *Through the Looking-Glass and what Alice found there*, followed in 1871. Carroll continued to produce mathematical treatises, narrative poems and short stories until his death in Guildford on 14 January 1898.

Jabberwocky – Lewis Carroll

The first verse of 'Jabberwocky' was written in 1855 as a parody of Anglo-Saxon poetry. The bulk of the poem was composed while Carroll was staying with his cousins, the Misses Wilcox, at Whitburn near Sunderland. During a game of verse-making there one evening, Carroll contributed 'Jabberwocky'. The poem that had its roots in the scribblings of the twenty-three-year-old Dodgson was integrated into *Through the Looking-Glass and what Alice found there*.

In *Misch Masch*, the periodical he wrote for the amusement of his family, Carroll offered an interpretation of the first stanza. (The spelling of some words was refined later.) The basic meaning of the first stanza is:

'It was four o'clock in the afternoon, and the smooth, active, cheese-eating, long-legged, horned badgers were scratching and boring holes in the rain-soaked hill side. The wingless, veal-eating parrots who nest under sun-dials were unhappy and the smooth green-bodied land-turtles that walked on their knees and lived on swallows and oysters were shrieking.'

In the early 1890s a school wrote to Carroll asking if they might call their new magazine 'Jabberwok'. Carroll agreed, pointing out that the Anglo-Saxon word *wocer* means 'offspring' or 'fruit', while *jabber* means 'an excited or voluble discussion', making it an ideal title for a magazine.

3

JABBERWOCKY

'Twas brillig, and the slithy toves
   Did gyre and gimble in the wabe:
All mimsy were the borogoves,
   And the mome raths outgrabe.

'Beware the Jabberwock, my son!
   The jaws that bite, the claws that catch!
Beware the Jubjub bird, and shun
   The frumious Bandersnatch!'

He took his vorpal sword in hand:
   Long time the manxome foe he sought—
So rested he by the Tumtum tree,
   And stood awhile in thought.

And, as in uffish thought he stood,
   The Jabberwock, with eyes of flame,
Came whiffling through the tulgy wood,
   And burbled as it came!

One, two! One, two! And through and through
   The vorpal blade went snicker-snack!
He left it dead, and with its head
   He went galumphing back.

'And hast thou slain the Jabberwock?
  Come to my arms, my beamish boy!
O frabjous day! Callooh! Callay!'
  He chortled in his joy.

'Twas brillig, and the slithy toves
  Did gyre and gimble in the wabe:
All mimsy were the borogoves,
  And the mome raths outgrabe.

SIR JOHN BETJEMAN
1906–84

John Betjemann (note the extra 'n') was born on 28 August 1906 in London and was first educated at the local Highgate Junior School, where his teachers included T. S. Eliot. He then moved via the Dragon School in Oxford to Marlborough, where he met Louis MacNeice and Anthony Blunt, who went on to become the famous art historian and spy. Family holidays were spent each summer on the north Cornish coast, where he began his lifelong passion for Cornwall. Schoolboy taunts at his Germanic-sounding name during the First World War led to the dropping of the extra 'n', and it was as Betjeman that he went up to Magdalen College, Oxford. He detested his tutor, C. S. Lewis, and much preferred the charismatic don Maurice Bowra.

After leaving Oxford without a degree, Betjeman was briefly a schoolmaster. An increasingly popular poet and early television personality, he founded the Victorian Society in 1958 and published his long autobiographical poem *Summoned by Bells* in 1960. He was knighted in 1968, and appointed Poet Laureate in 1974. He died on 19 May 1984 in his beloved Cornwall, where he now lies buried in the churchyard at St Enodoc.

Diary of a Church Mouse – John Betjeman

'Diary of a Church Mouse' was first published in *Poems in the Porch* in 1954, one of six poems written specifically for speaking on the wireless at the request of the Reverend Martin Wilson. Wilson was, at the time, Director of Religious Broadcasting for the Western Region at the BBC. A deluge of letters asking for copies led to the publication of the six poems, with Betjeman protesting '. . . in order to compensate for the shortcoming of the verse, I have prevailed on my friend, Mr John Piper, to provide the illustrations'.

Betjeman seemed bewildered by the durability and popularity of what he considered to be a piece of light verse written to order.

4

DIARY OF A CHURCH MOUSE
(Lines, written to order on a set subject, to be
spoken on the wireless.)

Here among long-discarded cassocks,
Damp stools, and half-split open hassocks,
Here where the Vicar never looks
I nibble through old service books.
Lean and alone I spend my days
Behind this Church of England baize.
I share my dark forgotten room
With two oil-lamps and half a broom.
The cleaner never bothers me,
So here I eat my frugal tea.
My bread is sawdust mixed with straw;
My jam is polish for the floor.
    Christmas and Easter may be feasts
For congregations and for priests,
And so may Whitsun. All the same,
They do not fill my meagre frame.
For me the only feast at all
Is Autumn's Harvest Festival,
When I can satisfy my want
With ears of corn around the font.
I climb the eagle's brazen head
To burrow through a loaf of bread.
I scramble up the pulpit stair

And gnaw the marrows hanging there.
   It is enjoyable to taste
These items ere they go to waste,
But how annoying when one finds
That other mice with pagan minds
Come into church my food to share
Who have no proper business there.
Two field mice who have no desire
To be baptized, invade the choir.
A large and most unfriendly rat
Comes in to see what we are at.
He says he thinks there is no God
And yet he comes . . . it's rather odd.
This year he stole a sheaf of wheat
(It screened our special preacher's seat),
And prosperous mice from fields away
Come in to hear the organ play,
And under cover of its notes
Ate through the altar's sheaf of oats.
A Low Church mouse, who thinks that I
Am too papistical, and High,
Yet somehow doesn't think it wrong
To munch through Harvest Evensong,
While I, who starve the whole year through,
Must share my food with rodents who
Except at this time of the year
Not once inside the church appear.
   Within the human world I know
Such goings-on could not be so,
For human beings only do

What their religion tells them to.
They read the Bible every day
And always, night and morning, pray,
And just like me, the good church mouse,
Worship each week in God's own house,
    But all the same it's strange to me
How very full the church can be
With people I don't see at all
Except at Harvest Festival.

HILAIRE BELLOC
1870–1953

Belloc was born near Paris of a French father and an English mother. The Franco-Prussian War of 1870–1 resulted in the destruction of the Belloc family property, and the future writer and his parents fled to London.

After his mother's death in 1891 Belloc led a semi-nomadic existence, lecturing across America and publishing books on touring France by bicycle. Sussex has already laid claim to being his spiritual home, and it was to Slindon in West Sussex that Belloc, his wife Elodie and their growing family moved in 1905. Despite his opponent's slogan, 'Don't Vote for a Frenchman and a Catholic!', Belloc took Salford for the Liberals at the 1906 election and was to remain an MP for some years. He later left the Liberals and teamed up with his great friend G. K. Chesterton to form what Shaw dubbed the one entity 'Chesterbelloc' in their many ideological disputes.

A prolific author, Belloc published 153 books during his lifetime. He is probably best remembered for his *Cautionary Tales*.

In 1906 he bought 'Kingsand' at Shipley in Sussex, complete with a working mill and five acres of land, for one thousand pounds, where he lived until his death.

Matilda – Hilaire Belloc

'Matilda' first saw the light of day in Belloc's *Cautionary Tales for Children*, published in 1907, and 'designed for the admonitions of children between the ages of eight and fourteen years'. Published by Eveleigh Nash with pictures by Basil Blackwood, this was the Anglophile's twenty-fourth book in eleven years. Belloc would have frustrated the media had he lived in the 1990s, for he wore many hats ... at the time of *Cautionary Tales* he was Liberal MP for Salford, but still managed to delight in the make-believe and sometimes frightening world of 'Henry King', 'Charles Augustus Fortescue' and 'Matilda'.

Sales of *Cautionary Tales* were helped considerably by the statuesque Sussex contralto Clara Butt who performed them the length and breadth of the country. Belloc's widow once told her, 'For the first time I have heard my dear husband's song sung as he would have wished to hear it'. The singer performed with equal passion for Gounod, Belloc and Queen Victoria.

5

MATILDA

WHO TOLD LIES, AND WAS BURNED TO DEATH

Matilda told such Dreadful Lies,
It made one Gasp and Stretch one's Eyes;
Her Aunt, who, from her Earliest Youth,
Had kept a Strict Regard for Truth,
Attempted to Believe Matilda:
The effort very nearly killed her,
And would have done so, had not She
Discovered this Infirmity.
For once, towards the Close of Day,
Matilda, growing tired of play,
And finding she was left alone,
Went tiptoe to the Telephone
And summoned the Immediate Aid
Of London's Noble Fire-Brigade.
Within an hour the Gallant Band
Were pouring in on every hand,
From Putney, Hackney Downs, and Bow.
With Courage high and Hearts a-glow,
They galloped, roaring through the Town,
'Matilda's House is Burning Down!'
Inspired by British Cheers and Loud
Proceeding from the Frenzied Crowd,
They ran their ladders through a score
Of windows on the Ball Room Floor;

And took Peculiar Pains to Souse
The Pictures up and down the House,
Until Matilda's Aunt succeeded
In showing them they were not needed;
And even then she had to pay
To get the Men to go away!

It happened that a few Weeks later
Her Aunt was off to the Theatre
To see that Interesting Play
The Second Mrs Tanqueray.
She had refused to take her Niece
To hear this Entertaining Piece:
A Deprivation Just and Wise
To Punish her for Telling Lies.
That Night a Fire *did* break out—
You should have heard Matilda Shout!
You should have heard her Scream and Bawl,
And throw the window up and call
To People passing in the Street—
(The rapidly increasing Heat
Encouraging her to obtain
Their confidence) – but all in vain!
For every time She shouted 'Fire!'
They only answered 'Little Liar!'
And therefore when her Aunt returned,
Matilda, and the House, were Burned.

THOMAS HARDY
1840–1928

Hardy was born on 2 June 1840 in Higher Bockhampton near Dorchester, the son of a builder and of a mother who worked in domestic service. While his father, a gifted musician, taught Hardy to play the violin, he was encouraged by his mother to pursue his literary ambitions. He left school in Dorchester at the age of sixteen to become apprenticed to a London architect, and in 1868, while on an architectural mission to Cornwall, met Emma Gifford. Six years later, a successful novelist, he could afford to abandon architecture and marry Emma. For three years from 1878 the Hardys lived in Tooting in London, mixing with literary notables including Browning, Tennyson, Henry James and Matthew Arnold.

In 1887 the Hardys returned to the countryside – to the house that he had designed near Dorchester. After the critical drubbing he received for *Tess of the D'Urbervilles* (1891) and *Jude the Obscure* (1895) Hardy returned to poetry, his first love. In 1912 Emma died and about the same time Hardy found himself restored to favour. He was awarded honorary degrees from both Oxford and Cambridge, was made a Fellow of the Royal Society of Literature and given the Order of Merit. When he died, on 11 January 1928, his heart was buried with his parents and Emma at Stinsford in Dorset, while his other remains rest in Westminster Abbey – a decision taken by his second wife, Florence.

The Ruined Maid – Thomas Hardy

Although the name of Hardy is synonymous with Wessex, 'The Ruined Maid' was written at Westbourne Park Villas in London in 1866. He was twenty-six when he wrote it, and just two years away from meeting Emma Gifford.

Poetry fairly poured out of Hardy during 1866, his works including 'The Hap', 'In Vision I Roamed', 'At a Bridal, Postponement', 'A Confession to a Friend in Trouble', 'Her Dilemma', 'Revulsion', and 'She to Him'.

6

THE RUINED MAID

'O 'Melia, my dear, this does everything crown!
Who could have supposed I should meet you in Town?
And whence such fair garments, such prosperi-ty?'—
'O didn't you know I'd been ruined?' said she.

—'You left us in tatters, without shoes or socks,
Tired of digging potatoes, and spudding up docks;
And now you've gay bracelets and bright feathers three!'—
'Yes: that's how we dress when we're ruined,' said she.

—'At home in the barton you said "thee" and "thou",
And "thik oon", and "theäs oon", and "t'other"; but now
Your talking quite fits 'ee for high compa-ny!'—
'Some polish is gained with one's ruin,' said she.

—'Your hands were like paws then, your face blue
    and bleak
But now I'm bewitched by your delicate cheek,
And your little gloves fit as on any la-dy!'—
'We never do work when we're ruined,' said she.

—'You used to call home-life a hag-ridden dream,
And you'd sigh, and you'd sock; but at present you seem
To know not of megrims or melancho-ly!'—
'True. One's pretty lively when ruined,' said she.

—'I wish I had feathers, a fine sweeping gown,
And a delicate face, and could strut about Town!'—
'My dear – a raw country girl, such as you be,
Cannot quite expect that. You ain't ruined,' said she.

The Walrus and the Carpenter – Lewis Carroll

The poem is from the Tweedledum and Tweedledee chapter of *Through the Looking-Glass and what Alice found there*, where it is recited by Tweedledee to Alice. Carroll uses the metre of Thomas Hood's murder poem 'The Dream of Eugene Mann' for the piece. Strangely, the most-quoted lines of the poem are the first four lines of stanza eleven, unlike most poems, where the opening is the most familiar. When Carroll gave the manuscript to Tenniel, his illustrator, he offered him the choice of depicting a carpenter, a baronet or a butterfly, as each were three-syllable words that would fit the poem – proof that he wasn't overly precious about it.

In Carroll's poem the oysters are eaten and that's an end to it, but the edible bivalve molluscs were allowed their revenge in Savile Clark's operetta *Alice*, where a bunch of ghostly oysters reappears to reprove the Walrus and the Carpenter, and stamp upon their chests when they sleep!

7

THE WALRUS AND THE CARPENTER

The sun was shining on the sea,
    Shining with all his might:
He did his very best to make
    The billows smooth and bright—
And this was odd, because it was
    The middle of the night.

The moon was shining sulkily,
    Because she thought the sun
Had got no business to be there
    After the day was done—
'It's very rude of him,' she said,
    'To come and spoil the fun!'

The sea was wet as wet could be,
    The sands were dry as dry.
You could not see a cloud, because
    No cloud was in the sky:
No birds were flying overhead—
    There were no birds to fly.

The Walrus and the Carpenter
    Were walking close at hand:
They wept like anything to see
    Such quantities of sand:
'If this were only cleared away,'
    They said, 'it would be grand!'

'If seven maids with seven mops
  Swept it for half a year,
Do you suppose,' the Walrus said,
  'That they could get it clear?'
'I doubt it,' said the Carpenter,
  And shed a bitter tear.

'O Oysters, come and walk with us!'
  The Walrus did beseech.
'A pleasant walk, a pleasant talk,
  Along the briny beach:
We cannot do with more than four,
  To give a hand to each.'

The eldest Oyster looked at him,
  But never a word he said:
The eldest Oyster winked his eye,
  And shook his heavy head—
Meaning to say he did not choose
  To leave the oyster-bed.

But four young Oysters hurried up,
  All eager for the treat:
Their coats were brushed, their faces washed,
  Their shoes were clean and neat—
And this was odd, because you know,
  They hadn't any feet.

Four other Oysters followed them,
　　And yet another four;
And thick and fast they came at last,
　　And more, and more, and more—
All hopping through the frothy waves,
　　And scrambling to the shore.

The Walrus and the Carpenter
　　Walked on a mile or so,
And then they rested on a rock
　　Conveniently low:
And all the little Oysters stood
　　And waited in a row.

'The time has come,' the Walrus said,
　　'To talk of many things:
Of shoes – and ships – and sealing wax—
　　Of cabbages – and kings—
And why the sea is boiling hot—
　　And whether pigs have wings.'

'But wait a bit,' the Oysters cried,
　　'Before we have our chat;
For some of us are out of breath,
　　And all of us are fat!'
'No hurry!' said the Carpenter.
　　They thanked him much for that.

'A loaf of bread,' the Walrus said,
　'Is what we chiefly need:
Pepper and vinegar besides
　Are very good indeed—
Now, if you're ready, Oysters dear
　We can begin to feed.'

'But not on us!' the Oysters cried,
　Turning a little blue.
'After such kindness, that would be
　A dismal thing to do!'
'The night is fine,' the Walrus said,
　'Do you admire the view?

'It was so kind of you to come!
　And you are very nice!'
The Carpenter said nothing but
　'Cut us another slice.
I wish you were not quite so deaf—
　I've had to ask you twice!'

'It seems a shame,' the Walrus said,
　'To play them such a trick.
After we've brought them out so far,
　And made them trot so quick!'
The Carpenter said nothing but
　'The butter's spread too thick!'

'I weep for you,' the Walrus said:
  'I deeply sympathize.'
With sobs and tears he sorted out
  Those of the largest size,
Holding his pocket-handkerchief
  Before his streaming eyes.

'O Oysters,' said the Carpenter,
  'You've had a pleasant run!
Shall we be trotting home again!'
  But answer came there none—
And this was scarcely odd, because
  They'd eaten every one.

The Village Choir – Anonymous

Tennyson's famous poem 'The Charge of the Light Brigade' has inspired many parodies since it was first written. The parodists were obviously inspired by the rhythm of those often quoted opening lines:

> *Half a league, half a league,*
> *Half a league onward,*
> *All in the valley of Death*
> *Rode the six hundred.*

A number of different versions were sent to me by Classic *f*M listeners, and this one proved the most popular.

8

THE VILLAGE CHOIR

Half a bar, half a bar,
Half a bar onward!
Into an awful ditch
Choir and precentor hitch,
Into a mess of pitch,
    They led the Old Hundred.
Trebles to right of them,
Tenors to left of them,
Basses in front of them,
    Bellowed and thundered.
Oh, that precentor's look,
When the sopranos took
Their own time and hook
    From the Old Hundred!

Screeched all the trebles here,
Boggled the tenors there,
Raising the parson's hair,
    While his mind wandered;
Theirs not to reason why
This psalm was pitched too high:
Theirs but to gasp and cry
    Out the Old Hundred.
Trebles to right of them,
Tenors to left of them.

Basses in front of them,
   Bellowed and thundered.
Stormed they with shout and yell,
Not wise they sang nor well,
Drowning the sexton's bell,
   While all the church wondered.

Dire the precentor's glare,
Flashed his pitchfork in air
Sounding fresh keys to bear
   Out the Old Hundred.
Swiftly he turned his back,
Reached he his hat from rack,
Then from the screaming pack,
   Himself he sundered.
Tenors to right of him,
Tenors to left of him,
Dischords behind him,
   Bellowed and thundered.
Oh, the wild howls they wrought:
Right to the end they fought!
Some tune they sang, but not,
   Not the Old Hundred.

T. S. ELIOT
1888–1965

Thomas Stearns Eliot was born in St Louis, Missouri, on 26 September 1888, the seventh and last child of a wealthy businessman. In 1906 Eliot went up to Harvard. He also studied at the Sorbonne in Paris and at the University of Marburg in Germany, and in 1914 he arrived in Britain to continue his studies at Merton College, Oxford. He wrote poetry while earning a living as a schoolmaster: one of his pupils at Highgate School in North London was the young John Betjeman, who presented Eliot with some of his very early works.

At the suggestion of his fellow expatriate poet, Ezra Pound, Eliot decided to settle in England, and in the summer of 1915 he married Vivien Haigh-Wood. Two years later he joined Lloyds Bank, from which he was rescued by the efforts of supporters such as Virginia Woolf, who secured him a job at the publishers Faber and Faber.

In 1927 Eliot became a British citizen and announced his conversion to Anglo-Catholicism. After the Second World War Eliot turned to the theatre, writing poetic dramas such as *The Cocktail Party* and *The Family Reunion*. In 1965, the year of his death, he was awarded the Order of Merit and the Nobel Prize for Literature.

Macavity: The Mystery Cat – T. S. Eliot

Old Possum's Book of Practical Cats by T. S. Eliot contains fifteen feline poems, Macavity being the tenth.

The book's continued popularity was guaranteed when Andrew Lloyd Webber adapted it, with additional lyrics by Trevor Nunn and Richard Stilgoe, for a new musical: *Cats*. *Cats* opened at the New London Theatre on 11 May 1981, the original cast including Brian Blessed, Bonnie Langford, Paul Nicholas, Sarah Brightman, Elaine Paige and Wayne Sleep. The musical is still going strong seventeen years on, and judging by your votes so are T. S. Eliot's original poems.

9

MACAVITY: THE MYSTERY CAT

Macavity's a Mystery Cat: he's called the Hidden Paw—
For he's the master criminal who can defy the Law.
He's the bafflement of Scotland Yard, the Flying Squad's
   despair:
For when they reach the scene of crime – *Macavity's
   not there*!

Macavity, Macavity, there's no one like Macavity,
He's broken every human law, he breaks the law of
   gravity.
His powers of levitation would make a fakir stare,
And when you reach the scene of crime – *Macavity's
   not there*!
You may seek him in the basement, you may look up in
   the air—
But I tell you once and once again, *Macavity's not there*!

Macavity's a ginger cat, he's very tall and thin;
You would know him if you saw him, for his eyes are
   sunken in.
His brow is deeply lined with thought, his head is highly
   domed;
His coat is dusty from neglect, his whiskers are uncombed.
He sways his head from side to side, with movements
   like a snake;
And when you think he's half asleep, he's always wide
   awake.

Macavity, Macavity, there's no one like Macavity,
For he's a fiend in feline shape, a monster of depravity.
You may meet him in a by-street, you may see him in
the square—
But when a crime's discovered, then *Macavity's not
there*!

He's outwardly respectable. (They say he cheats at cards.)
And his footprints are not found in any file of Scotland
Yard's.
And when the larder's looted, or the jewel-case is rifled,
Or when the milk is missing, or another Peke's been
stifled,
Or the greenhouse glass is broken, and the trellis past
repair—
Ay, there's the wonder of the thing! *Macavity's not
there*!

And when the Foreign Office find a Treaty's gone astray,
Or the Admiralty lose some plans and drawings by
the way,
There may be a scrap of paper in the hall or on the
stair—
But it's useless to investigate – *Macavity's not there*!
And when the loss has been disclosed, the Secret Service
say:
It *must* have been Macavity!' – but he's a mile away.
You'll be sure to find him resting, or a-licking of his
thumbs,
Or engaged in doing complicated long division sums.

Macavity, Macavity, there's no one like Macavity,
There never was a Cat of such deceitfulness and suavity.
He always has an alibi, and one or two to spare:
At whatever time the deed took place – MACAVITY WASN'T
    THERE!
And they say that all the Cats whose wicked deeds are
    widely known
(I might mention Mungojerrie, I might mention
    Griddlebone)
Are nothing more than agents for the Cat who all the
    time
Just controls their operations: the Napoleon of Crime!

G. K. CHESTERTON
1874–1936

———— ⊗⊗⊗ ————

Gilbert Keith Chesterton was born in Kensington, West London, on 29 May 1874, the son of an estate agent. He attended St Paul's School, then enrolled at the Slade School of Art before reading English Literature at London University, which he left without taking a degree. He began his career as a journalist by contributing to the *Spectator*, and was already a well-known figure when his opposition to the Boer War brought him into contact with Hilaire Belloc, and the two became close friends. They shared a distaste for, amongst other things, women's suffrage and agnosticism, which brought them into conflict with such notables as Shaw and H. G. Wells. In 1905 Chesterton began a weekly column for the *Illustrated London News* which ran, virtually without interruption, until 1930.

A large man, Chesterton seemed to grow more out-sized and more absent-minded every year. On one famous occasion, on his way to give one of his many talks, he telegraphed his wife with the plea: 'Am in Market Harborough – where ought I to be?' For all the essays, poems and articles which poured from his pen, Chesterton is probably best remembered for the creation of the clerical sleuth Father Brown. When he died at his home in Beaconsfield, Buckinghamshire, on 14 June 1936, Belloc observed that 'Chesterton will never occur again'.

10

THE ROLLING ENGLISH ROAD

Before the Roman came to Rye or out to Severn strode,
The rolling English drunkard made the rolling English road.
A reeling road, a rolling road, that rambles round the shire,
And after him the parson ran, the sexton and the squire;
A merry road, a mazy road, and such as we did tread
That night we went to Birmingham by way of Beachy Head.

I knew no harm of Bonaparte and plenty of the Squire,
And for to fight the Frenchmen I did not much desire;
But I did bash their baggonets because they came arrayed
To straighten out the crooked road an English
    drunkard made,
Where you and I went down the lane with ale-mugs in
    our hands,
The night we went to Glastonbury by way of Goodwin
    Sands.

His sins they were forgiven him; or why do flowers run
Behind him; and the hedges all strengthening in the sun?
The wild thing went from left to right and knew not which
    was which
But the wild rose was above him when they found him
    in the ditch
God pardon us, nor harden us; we did not see so clear
The night we went to Bannockburn by way of Brighton Pier.

My friends, we will not go again or ape an ancient rage,
Or stretch the folly of our youth to be the shame of age,
But walk with clearer eyes and ears this path that wandereth,
And see undrugged in evening light the decent inn of death;
For there is good news yet to hear and fine things to be seen,
Before we go to Paradise by way of Kensal Green.

The Pobble who has no Toes – Edward Lear

'The Pobble who has no Toes' made his first appearance in Lear's 1877 book *Laughable Lyrics*, along with 'The Dong with a Luminous Nose' and 'The Quangle Wangle's Hat'. The definition of Lear's word runcible is in question again, as a three-pronged fork shaped like a spoon could hardly apply to Aunt Jobiska's Runcible Cat with crimson whiskers!

11

THE POBBLE WHO HAS NO TOES

The Pobble who has no toes
    Had once as many as we;
When they said, 'Some day you may lose them all;'—
He replied, – 'Fish fiddle de-dee!'
And his Aunt Jobiska made him drink,
Lavender water tinged with pink,
For she said, 'The World in general knows
There's nothing so good for a Pobble's toes!'
The Pobble who has no toes,
    Swam across the Bristol Channel;
But before he set out he wrapped his nose
    In a piece of scarlet flannel.
For his Aunt Jobiska said, 'No harm
Can come to his toes if his nose is warm;
And it's perfectly known that a Pobble's toes
Are safe, – provided he minds his nose.'
The Pobble swam fast and well,
    And when boats or ships came near him
He tinkledy-binkledy-winkled a bell,
    So that all the world could hear him.
And all the Sailors and Admirals cried,
When they saw him nearing the further side,—
'He has gone to fish, for his Aunt Jobiska's
Runcible Cat with crimson whiskers!'
But before he touched the shore,

The shore of the Bristol Channel,
A sea-green Porpoise carried away
    His wrapper of scarlet flannel.
And when he came to observe his feet,
Formerly garnished with toes so neat,
His face at once became forlorn
On perceiving that all his toes were gone!
And nobody ever knew
    From that dark day to the present,
Whoso had taken the Pobble's toes,
    In a manner so far from pleasant.
Whether the shrimps or crawfish gray,
Or crafty Mermaids stole them away—
Nobody knew; and nobody knows
How the Pobble was robbed of his twice five toes!
The Pobble who has no toes
    Was placed in a friendly Bark,
And they rowed him back, and carried him up,
    To his Aunt Jobiska's Park.
And she made him a feast at his earnest wish
Of eggs and buttercups fried with fish;—
And she said, – 'It's a fact the whole world knows,
That Pobbles are happier without their toes.'

How to get on in Society – John Betjeman

In 1949 Betjeman became Literary Advisor/Editor of *Time & Tide* magazine, which he always called *Tame & Tade*! He wrote the five verses of 'How to get on in Society' as a competition for the 29 December 1951 edition of the magazine, inviting readers to compile a final stanza. The winner was 'H.M.B', who added:

> *Your pochette's on the pouffe by the cake stand*
> *Beneath your fur-fabric coatie*
> *Now before we remove to the study*
> *Let me pass you these chocs from Paris*

12

HOW TO GET ON IN SOCIETY

Phone for the fish-knives, Norman,
As cook is a little unnerved;
You kiddies have crumpled the serviettes
And I must have things daintily served.

Are the requisites all in the toilet?
The frills round the cutlets can wait
Till the girl has replenished the cruets
And switched on the logs in the grate.

It's ever so close in the lounge dear,
But the vestibule's comfy for tea
And Howard is out riding on horseback,
So do come and take some with me.

Now here is a fork for your pastries,
And do use the couch for your feet;
I know what I wanted to ask you—
Is trifle sufficient for sweet?

Milk and then just as it comes dear?
I'm afraid the preserve's full of stones;
Beg pardon, I'm soiling the doileys
With afternoon tea-cakes and scones.

JENNY JOSEPH
born 1932

———— ❧❧❧ ————

Jenefer Ruth Joseph was born in Birmingham on 7 May 1932 and read English at St Hilda's College, Oxford. She then worked as a reporter before moving to South Africa for two years. Her first collection of poems was published in 1960, but she still had to make a living, running a London pub from 1969 to 1972 and then teaching and lecturing in extra-mural and adult education. She has continued to write award-winning verse through the subsequent decades, as well as turning to fiction, for which she received the James Tait Black Memorial Award in 1986. Commenting on her own work, she has observed that 'It is usually easier for a writer to talk about what he or she is doing "now" or "next" than about what has been done.'

13

WARNING

When I am an old woman I shall wear purple
With a red hat which doesn't go, and doesn't suit me,
And I shall spend my pension on brandy and summer
   gloves
And satin sandals, and say we've no money for butter.
I shall sit down on the pavement when I'm tired
And gobble up samples in shops and press alarm bells
And run my stick along the public railings
And make up for the sobriety of my youth.
I shall go out in my slippers in the rain
And pick the flowers in other people's gardens
And learn to spit.

You can wear terrible shirts and grow more fat
And eat three pounds of sausages at a go
Or only bread and pickle for a week
And hoard pens and pencils and beermats and things
   in boxes.

But now we must have clothes that keep us dry
And pay our rent and not swear in the street
And set a good example for the children.
We must have friends to dinner and read the papers.

But maybe I ought to practise a little now?
So people who know me are not too shocked and
  surprised
When suddenly I am old, and start to wear purple.

Father William – Lewis Carroll

'Father William' parodies 'The Old Man's Comforts and how He Gained Them', written by Richard Southey, the Poet Laureate from 1814 until his death in 1843. Carroll attended Christ Church, Oxford, and Southey, some fifty years before him in 1793, almost did! In the end he had to settle for Balliol. Father William appears in chapter five of *Alice's Adventures in Wonderland* – 'Advice from a Caterpillar'. The insect tells her to 'Repeat you are old, Father William'. Alice then folds her arms and begins:

14

FATHER WILLIAM

'You are old, Father William,' the young man said,
  'And your hair has become very white;
And yet you incessantly stand on your head—
  Do you think, at your age, it is right?'

'In my youth,' Father William replied to his son,
  'I feared it might injure the brain;
But, now that I'm perfectly sure I have none,
  Why, I do it again and again.'

'You are old,' said the youth, 'as I mentioned before,
  And have grown most uncommonly fat;
Yet you turned a back-somersault in at the door—
  Pray, what is the reason of that?'

'In my youth,' said the sage, as he shook his grey locks,
  'I kept all my limbs very supple
By the use of this ointment – one shilling the box—
  Allow me to sell you a couple?'

'You are old,' said the youth, 'and your jaws are too weak
  For anything tougher than suet;
Yet you finished the goose, with the bones and the beak—
  Pray, how did you manage to do it?'

'In my youth,' said his father, 'I took to the law,
   And argued each case with my wife;
And the muscular strength, which it gave to my jaw,
   Has lasted the rest of my life.'

'You are old,' said the youth, 'one would hardly suppose
   That your eye was as steady as ever;
Yet you balanced an eel on the end of your nose—
   What made you so awfully clever?'

'I have answered three questions, and that is enough,'
   Said his father; 'don't give yourself airs!
Do you think I can listen all day to such stuff?
   Be off, or I'll kick you down stairs!'

PAM AYRES
born 1947

⸺ ◈◈◈ ⸺

It was November 1975 when Pam Ayres made the first of her multi-winning appearances on the ITV talent show *Opportunity Knocks*, and this proved to be the start of a unique career.

Pam Ayres always wanted to be a writer. At school she shone brilliantly at English and art, but was pretty useless at everything else. The youngest of a family of six children, she was born in Stanford-in-the-Vale, Berkshire, during the long, cold winter of 1947. After leaving school, Pam joined the Civil Service as a clerical assistant, a job in which she soon lost interest, and which prompted her to join the Women's Royal Air Force. It was while Pam was in the WRAF that she developed her love of singing and acting, and slowly the wild idea emerged that she would like to be an 'entertainer', although she had no idea how to go about it.

However, on leaving the WRAF, Pam set out to achieve her ambition. By this time her poems and verses had become a hobby, to be written and performed for the local folk club in Oxfordshire, where she had returned to live and work as a secretary. In 1974 a friend arranged for her to go to the local radio station, BBC Radio Oxford, to read one of her poems. Pam's first broadcast for Radio Oxford, in 1974, was selected for BBC Radio 4's *Pick of the Week* and subsequently repeated on the 1974 *Pick of the Year*, by which time Radio Oxford has asked Pam to return and recite some more of her poems.

After receiving rejection slips from several well-known publishers, Pam decided to publish her poems herself, and thus was printed *The Entire Collection (Eight) of Masterpieces by Pam Ayres, Famous Poet and Washer of Jamjars*, which sold very successfully in her local area. In 1975, after much prodding from friends, Pam decided to audition for television's *Opportunity Knocks*.

Since then Pam Ayres has appeared on virtually every major TV show in the UK, has had her own TV series, and filmed Christmas TV specials in Hong Kong and Canada. She has published six books of poems. Sales of these have exceeded two million worldwide. She has recorded seven record albums and has silver, gold and platinum records.

Pam Ayres is married to concert agent and theatre producer Dudley Russell, and they have two sons, William and James. The family lives in the Cotswolds, where Pam is a keen (and knowledgeable) gardener, chicken-keeper and beekeeper.

15

OH, I WISH I'D LOOKED AFTER ME TEETH

Oh, I wish I'd looked after me teeth,
    And spotted the perils beneath,
All the toffees I chewed,
    And the sweet sticky food,
Oh, I wish I'd looked after me teeth.

I wish I'd been that much more willin'
    When I had more tooth there than fillin'
To give-up gobstoppers,
    From respect to me choppers,
And to buy something else with me shillin'.

When I think of the lollies I licked,
    And the liquorice allsorts I picked,
Sherbet dabs, big and little,
    All that hard peanut brittle,
My conscience gets horribly pricked.

My mother, she told me no end,
    'If you got a tooth, you got a friend.'
I was young then, and careless,
    My toothbrush was hairless,
I never had much time to spend.

Oh I showed them the toothpaste all right,
　　I flashed it about late at night,
But up-and-down brushin'
　　And pokin' and fussin'
Didn't seem worth the time – I could bite!

If I'd known I was paving the way
　　To cavities, caps and decay,
The murder of fillin's
　　Injections and drillin's,
I'd have thrown all me sherbet away.

So I lay in the old dentist's chair,
　　And I gaze up his nose in despair,
And his drill it do whine,
　　In these molars of mine.
'Two amalgum,' he'll say, 'for in there.'

How I laughed at my mother's false teeth,
　　As they foamed in the waters beneath.
But now comes the reckonin'
　　It's *me* they are beckonin'
Oh, I *wish* I'd looked after me teeth.

The Dong with a Luminous Nose – Edward Lear

'The Dong with a Luminous Nose' appears in Lear's *Laughable Lyrics*, published in 1877. Companion poems in the books include 'The Pobble who has no Toes' and 'The Quangle Wangle's Hat'.

16

THE DONG WITH A LUMINOUS NOSE

When awful darkness and silence reign
Over the great Gromboolian plain,
   Through the long, long wintry nights;—
When the angry breakers roar
As they beat on the rocky shore;—
   When Storm-clouds brood on the towering heights
Of the Hills of the Chankly Bore:—
Then, through the vast and gloomy dark,
There moves what seems a fiery spark,
   A lonely spark with silvery rays
   Piercing the coal-black night,—
   A Meteor strange and bright:—
Hither and thither the vision strays,
   A single lurid light.

Slowly it wanders, – pauses, – creeps,—
Anon it sparkles, – flashes and leaps;
And ever as onward it gleaming goes
A light on the Bong-tree stems it throws.
And those who watch at that midnight hour
From Hall or Terrace, or lofty Tower,
Cry, as the wild light passes along,—
     'The Dong! – the Dong!
  The wandering Dong through the forest goes!
    The Dong! the Dong!
  The Dong with a luminous Nose!'

Long years ago
  The Dong was happy and gay,
Till he fell in love with a Jumbly Girl
  Who came to those shores one day,
For the Jumblies came in a sieve, they did,—
Landing at eve near the Zemmery Fidd
    Where the Oblong Oysters grow,
  And the rocks are smooth and gray.
And all the woods and the valleys rang
With the Chorus they daily and nightly sang,—
    'Far and few, far and few,
    Are the lands where the Jumblies live;
    Their heads are green, and their hands are blue
    And they went to sea in a sieve.'

Happily, happily passed those days!
    While the cheerful Jumblies staid;
  They danced in circlets all night long,
  To the plaintive pipe of the lively Dong,
    In moonlight, shine, or shade.
For day and night he was always there
By the side of the Jumbly Girl so fair,
With her sky-blue hands, and her sea-green hair.
Till the morning came of that hateful day
When the Jumblies sailed in their sieve away,
And the Dong was left on the cruel shore
Gazing – gazing for evermore,—
Ever keeping his weary eyes on
That pea-green sail on the far horizon,—
Singing the Jumbly Chorus still

As he sate all day on the grassy hill,—
> *'Far and few, far and few,*
> *Are the lands where the Jumblies live;*
> *Their heads are green, and their hands are blue,*
> *And they went to sea in a sieve.'*

But when the sun was low in the West,
The Dong arose and said;—
—'What little sense I once possessed
Has quite gone out of my head!'—
And since that day he wanders still
By lake and forest, marsh and hill,
Singing – 'O somewhere, in valley or plain
Might I find my Jumbly Girl again!
For ever I'll seek by lake and shore
Till I find my Jumbly Girl once more!'

Playing a pipe with silvery squeaks,
Since then his Jumbly Girl he seeks,
And because by night he could not see,
He gathered the bark of the Twangum Tree
On the flowery plain that grows.
And he wove him a wondrous Nose,—
A Nose as strange as a Nose could be!
Of vast proportions and painted red,
And tied with cords to the back of his head.
—In a hollow rounded space it ended
With a luminous Lamp within suspended,
All fenced about
With a bandage stout

To prevent the wind from blowing it out;—
And with holes all round to send the light,
In gleaming rays on the dismal night.

And now each night, and all night long,
Over those plains still roams the Dong;
And above the wail of the Chimp and Snipe
You may hear the squeak of his plaintive pipe
While ever he seeks, but seeks in vain
To meet with his Jumbly Girl again;
Lonely and wild – all night he goes,—
The Dong with a luminous Nose!
And all who watch at the midnight hour,
From Hall or Terrace, or lofty Tower,
Cry, as they trace the Meteor bright,
Moving along through the dreary night,—
   'This is the hour when forth he goes,
   The Dong with a luminous Nose!
   Yonder – over the plain he goes;
      He goes!
      He goes;
   The Dong with a luminous Nose!'

The Hunting of the Snark – Lewis Carroll

The last line of 'The Hunting of the Snark' occurred to the author while he was walking in Guildford in 1874, resulting in him writing the epic poem in order for him to explain it! The humorous odyssey, written between 1874 and 1876, has been the subject of much speculation as to the author's meaning, but as Carroll himself confessed, 'I'm very much afraid that I didn't mean anything but nonsense!' He was encouraged to complete the poem by a young girl called Gertrude Chataway, whom he'd met while on holiday in Sandown on the Isle of Wight in 1875.

He mischievously decided on April Fool's Day 1876 as the publication date, and despite a slow start, by 1908 it had been reprinted seventeen times.

A likely blueprint for 'Snark' was W. S. Gilbert's 'Bab Ballads', a copy of which was owned and cherished by Carroll.

17

from THE HUNTING OF THE SNARK
Fit the Second
The Bellman's Speech

The Bellman himself they all praised to the skies—
   Such a carriage, such ease and such grace!
Such solemnity, too! One could see he was wise,
   The moment one looked in his face!

He had bought a large map representing the sea,
   Without the least vestige of land:
And the crew were much pleased when they found
   it to be
   A map they could all understand.

'What's the good of Mercator's North Poles and Equators,
   Tropics, Zones, and Meridian Lines?'
So the Bellman would cry: and the crew would reply,
   'They are merely conventional signs!

'Other maps are such shapes, with their islands and capes!
   But we've got our brave Captain to thank'
(So the crew would protest) 'that he's bought us the best—
   A perfect and absolute blank!'

This was charming, no doubt: but they shortly found out
   That the Captain they trusted so well
Had only one notion for crossing the ocean,
   And that was to tingle his bell.

He was thoughtful and grave – but the orders he gave
   Were enough to bewilder a crew.
When he cried, 'Steer to starboard, but keep her head
   larboard!'
   What on earth was the helmsman to do?

Then the bowsprit got mixed with the rudder some-
times:
   A thing, as the Bellman remarked,
That frequently happens in tropical climes,
   When a vessel is, so to speak, 'snarked.'

But the principal failing occurred in the sailing,
   And the Bellman, perplexed and distressed,
Said he *had* hoped, at least, when the wind blew due
   East
   That the ship would *not* travel due West!

But the danger was past – they had landed at last,
   With their boxes, portmanteaus, and bags:
Yet at first sight the crew were not pleased with the
   view,
   Which consisted of chasms and crags.

The Bellman perceived that their spirits were low,
   And repeated in musical tone
Some jokes he had kept for a season of woe—
   But the crew would do nothing but groan.

He served out some grog with a liberal hand,
   And bade them sit down on the beach:
And they could not but own that their Captain looked
   grand,
   As he stood and delivered his speech.

'Friends, Romans, and countrymen, lend me your ears!'
   (They were all of them fond of quotations:
So they drank to his health, and they gave him three
   cheers,
   While he served out additional rations.)

'We have sailed many months, we have sailed many
   weeks
   (Four weeks to the month you may mark),
But never as yet ('tis your Captain who speaks)
   Have we caught the least glimpse of a Snark!

'We have sailed many weeks, we have sailed many
   days
   (Seven days to the week I allow),
But a Snark, on the which we might lovingly gaze,
   We have never beheld till now!

'Come, listen, my men, while I tell you again
    The five unmistakable marks
By which you may know, wheresoever you go,
    The warranted genuine Snarks.

'Let us take them in order. The first is the taste,
    Which is meagre and hollow, but crisp:
Like a coat that is rather too tight in the waist,
    With a flavour of Will-o'-the-wisp.

'Its habit of getting up late you'll agree
    That it carries too far, when I say
That it frequently breakfasts at five-o'clock tea,
    And dines on the following day.

'The third is its slowness in taking a jest,
    Should you happen to venture on one,
It will sigh like a thing that is deeply distressed:
    And it always looks grave at a pun.

'The fourth is its fondness for bathing-machines,
    Which it constantly carries about,
And believes that they add to the beauty of scenes—
    A sentiment open to doubt.

'The fifth is ambition. It next will be right
    To describe each particular batch:
Distinguishing those that have feathers, and bite,
    From those that have whiskers, and scratch.

'For, although common Snarks do no manner of harm,
  Yet, I feel it my duty to say,
Some are Boojums—' The Bellman broke off in alarm,
  For the Baker had fainted away.

The Jumblies – Edward Lear

'The Jumblies' first appeared in *Nonsense Songs* in 1871 with 'The Owl and the Pussy-cat'.

18

THE JUMBLIES

I

They went to sea in a Sieve, they did,
    In a Sieve they went to sea:
In spite of all their friends could say,
On a winter's morn, on a stormy day,
    In a Sieve they went to sea!
And when the Sieve turned round and round,
And every one cried, 'You'll all be drowned!'
They called aloud, 'Our Sieve ain't big,
But we don't care a button! we don't care a fig!
    In a Sieve we'll go to sea!'
        Far and few, far and few,
            Are the lands where the Jumblies live;
            Their heads are green, and their hands are blue,
                And they went to sea in a Sieve.

II

They sailed in a Sieve, they did,
    In a Sieve they sailed so fast,
With only a beautiful pea-green veil
Tied with a riband by way of a sail,
    To a small tobacco-pipe mast;
And every one said, who saw them go,
'O won't they be soon upset, you know!
For the sky is dark, and the voyage is long,

And happen what may, it's extremely wrong
   In a Sieve to sail so fast!'
      Far and few, far and few,
         Are the lands where the Jumblies live;
       Their heads are green, and their hands are blue,
         And they went to sea in a Sieve.

III

The water it soon came in, it did,
   The water it soon came in;
So to keep them dry, they wrapped their feet
In a pinky paper all folded neat,
   And they fastened it down with a pin.
And they passed the night in a crockery-jar,
And each of them said, 'How wise we are!
Though the sky be dark, and the voyage be long,
Yet we never can think we were rash or wrong,
   While round in our Sieve we spin!'
      Far and few, far and few,
         Are the lands where the Jumblies live;
       Their heads are green, and their hands are blue,
         And they went to sea in a Sieve.

IV

And all night long they sailed away;
   And when the sun went down,
They whistled and warbled a moony song
To the echoing sound of a coppery gong,
   In the shade of the mountains brown.
'O Timballo! How happy we are,

When we live in a sieve and a crockery-jar,
And all night long in the moonlight pale,
We sail away with a pea-green sail,
  In the shade of the mountains brown!'
    Far and few, far and few,
      Are the lands where the Jumblies live;
      Their heads are green, and their hands are blue,
        And they went to sea in a Sieve.

V

They sailed to the Western Sea, they did,
  To a land all covered with trees,
And they bought an Owl, and a useful Cart,
And a pound of Rice, and a Cranberry Tart,
  And a hive of silvery Bees.
And they bought a Pig, and some green Jack-daws,
And a lovely Monkey with lollipop paws,
And forty bottles of Ring-Bo-Ree,
  And no end of Stilton Cheese.
    Far and few, far and few,
      Are the lands where the Jumblies live;
      Their heads are green, and their hands are blue,
        And they went to sea in a Sieve.

VI

And in twenty years they all came back,
  In twenty years or more,
And every one said, 'How tall they've grown!
For they've been to the Lakes, and the Torrible Zone,
  And the hills of the Chankly Bore';

And they drank their health, and gave them a feast
Of dumplings made of beautiful yeast;
And every one said, 'If we only live,
We too will go to sea in a Sieve,—
  To the hills of the Chankly Bore!'
    Far and few, far and few,
      Are the lands where the Jumblies live;
     Their heads are green, and their hands are blue,
      And they went to sea in a Sieve.

Skimbleshanks: The Railway Cat – T. S. Eliot

The thirteenth of fifteen poems that comprise Eliot's *Old Possum's Book of Practical Cats*. In the original stage version of the musical *Cats* (see page 38, 'Macavity: The Mystery Cat' for details) the Skimbleshanks song was sung by Paul Nicholas.

19

SKIMBLESHANKS: THE RAILWAY CAT

There's a whisper down the line at 11.39
When the Night Mail's ready to depart,
Saying 'Skimble where is Skimble has he gone to hunt
 the thimble?
We must find him or the train can't start.'
All the guards and all the porters and the stationmaster's
 daughters
They are searching high and low,
Saying 'Skimble where is Skimble for unless he's very
 nimble
Then the Night Mail just can't go.'
At 11.42 then the signal's nearly due
And the passengers are frantic to a man—
Then Skimble will appear and he'll saunter to the rear:
He's been busy in the luggage van!
    He gives one flash of his glass-green eyes
        And the signal goes 'All Clear!'
    And we're off at last for the northern part
        Of the Northern Hemisphere!

You may say that by and large it is Skimble who's
 in charge
Of the Sleeping Car Express.
From the driver and the guards to the bagmen
 playing cards

He will supervise them all, more or less.
Down the corridor he paces and examines all the faces
Of the travellers in the First and in the Third;
He establishes control by a regular patrol
And he'd know at once if anything occurred.
He will watch you without winking and he sees what
   you are thinking
And it's certain that he doesn't approve
Of hilarity and riot, so the folk are very quiet
When Skimble is about and on the move.
   You can play no pranks with Skimbleshanks!
     He's a Cat that cannot be ignored;
  So nothing goes wrong on the Northern Mail
     When Skimbleshanks is aboard.

Oh it's very pleasant when you have found your little den
With your name written up on the door.
And the berth is very neat with a newly folded sheet
And there's not a speck of dust on the floor.
There is every sort of light – you can make it dark
   or bright;
There's a handle that you turn to make a breeze.
There's a funny little basin you're supposed to wash
   your face in
And a crank to shut the window if you sneeze.
Then the guard looks in politely and will ask you very
   brightly
'Do you like your morning tea weak or strong?'
But Skimble's just behind him and was ready to remind
   him,

For Skimble won't let anything go wrong.
  And when you creep into your cosy berth
    And pull up the counterpane,
  You ought to reflect that it's very nice
  To know that you won't be bothered by mice—
  You can leave all that to the Railway Cat,
    The Cat of the Railway Train!

In the watches of the night he is always fresh and
    bright;
Every now and then he has a cup of tea
With perhaps a drop of Scotch while he's keeping on
    the watch,
Only stopping here and there to catch a flea.
You were fast asleep at Crewe and so you never knew
That he was walking up and down the station;
You were sleeping all the while he was busy at Carlisle,
Where he greets the stationmaster with elation.
But you saw him at Dumfries, where he speaks to
    the police
If there's anything they ought to know about:
When you get to Gallowgate there you do not have
    to wait—
For Skimbleshanks will help you to get out!
  He gives you a wave of his long brown tail
    Which says: 'I'll see you again!
  You'll meet without fail on the Midnight Mail
    The cat of the Railway Train.'

KENNETH GRAHAME
1859–1932

Born in Edinburgh in 1859 into a family of devout Calvinists, Grahame lost his mother to scarlet fever when he was five years old, resulting in him being sent to live with his brothers and sisters at their grandmother's home in Berkshire.

Educated at St Edward's School, Oxford, his attempt to get into Oxford University was thwarted by relatives who thought a career in banking was a more suitable way forward.

His classic *The Golden Age* was published in 1895 with its continuation, *Dream Days*, coming out three years later, and receiving great praise from the likes of Swinburne. His finest hour was the children's story *The Wind in the Willows*, published in October 1908, featuring those endearing, much-loved and durable characters Rat, Badger, Toad and Mole. *The Wind in the Willows* was adapted as a stage play by both A. A Milne and Alan Bennett.

The Song of Mr Toad – Kenneth Grahame

From Grahame's children's classic *The Wind in the Willows*, 'The Song of Mr Toad', the stubborn, motorcar-loving amphibian, has proved to be a durable and much-loved piece of verse.

The Wind in the Willows evolved from stories that Grahame made up to entertain his son Alistair, about a mole, a toad, a water rat and a badger. The reviewers gave the book a hard time. *The Times Literary Supplement* referred to *The Wind in the Willows* as 'a book with hardly a smile in it, through which we wander in a state of perplexity ... The puzzle is for whom is the book intended? Grown up readers will find it monotonous and elusive; children will hope in vain for more fun.' Time is the most honest and unbiased critic, and in this case proved the Edwardian reviewers to be wide of the mark.

20

THE SONG OF MR TOAD

The world has held great Heroes,
  As history books have showed;
But never a name to go down to fame
  Compared with that of Toad!

The clever men at Oxford
  Know all that there is to be knowed,
But they none of them knew one half as much
  As intelligent Mr Toad!

The animals sat in the Ark and cried,
  Their tears in torrents flowed.
Who was it said, 'There's land ahead'?
  Encouraging Mr Toad!

The Army all saluted
  As they marched along the road.
Was it the King? Or Kitchener?
  No. It was Mr Toad!

The Queen and her Ladies-in-waiting
  Sat at the window and sewed.
She cried, 'Look! who's that *handsome* man?'
  They answered, 'Mr Toad.'

Hunter Trials – John Betjeman

Lady Betjeman told me that 'Hunter Trials' was written following a gymkhana in which the Betjemans' son Paul had ridden. John had also attended, but clearly didn't understand gymkhana terminology!

21

HUNTER TRIALS

It's awf'lly bad luck on Diana,
   Her ponies have swallowed their bits;
She fished down their throats with a spanner
   And frightened them all into fits.

So now she's attempting to borrow.
   Do lend her some bits, Mummy, *do*;
I'll lend her my own for to-morrow,
   But to-day *I'll* be wanting them too.

Just look at Prunella on Guzzle,
   The wizardest pony on earth;
Why doesn't she slacken his muzzle
   And tighten the breech in his girth?

I say, Mummy, there's Mrs Geyser
   And doesn't she look pretty sick?
I bet it's because Mona Lisa
   Was hit on the hock with a brick.

Miss Blewitt says Monica threw it,
   But Monica says it was Joan,
And Joan's very thick with Miss Blewitt,
   So Monica's sulking alone.

And Margaret failed in her paces,
　　Her withers got tied in a noose,
So her coronets caught in the traces
　　And now all her fetlocks are loose.

Oh, it's me now. I'm terribly nervous.
　　I wonder if Smudges will shy.
She's practically certain to swerve as
　　Her Pelham is over one eye.

Oh wasn't it naughty of Smudges?
　　Oh, Mummy, I'm sick with disgust.
She threw me in front of the Judges,
　　And my silly old collarbone's bust.

HILAIRE BELLOC

(see page 17 for biography)

THE HIPPOPOTAMUS

I shoot the Hippopotamus
With bullets made of platinum,
Because if I use leaden ones
His hide is sure to flatten 'em.

WILLIAM McGONAGALL
1825–1902

———— ∞∞∞ ————

Born in Edinburgh either in 1825 or 1830 (he claimed both dates!) to an Irish father, McGonagall's youth was spent on the island of South Ronaldsay in the Orkneys. At the age of eleven he moved with his family to Dundee, where he eventually became a handloom weaver. A keen amateur actor with an interest in the theatre and Shakespeare, he frequently joined visiting productions, taking the parts of Othello, Richard III, Hamlet and Macbeth. In 1877 he was, one day, gripped suddenly with an overwhelming desire to be a poet: '. . . all of a sudden my body got inflamed, and instantly I was seized with a strong desire to write poetry, so strong, in fact, that in imagination I thought I heard a voice crying in my ears – "write! write"!'

The following year his first book of poems was published, which included 'The Railway Bridge of the Silvery Tay'. Believing poetry to be his calling, he felt it his duty to travel and recite his works. Poverty was the result, with his wife Jean being forced to find work. A butt of the locals' humour in Dundee, he travelled to London, and more permanently to New York, before returning to Dundee.

He tried in vain to peddle his poems in Perth before going back to live in his native city, Edinburgh.

The Railway Bridge of The Silvery Tay – William McGonagall

Construction of the Tay Bridge began in 1874 and was completed in 1877 at the cost of £350,000. Officially it opened on 31 May 1878. It inspired the fifty-two-year-old William McGonagall to write 'The Railway Bridge of the Silvery Tay', and the Dundee press to proclaim him 'The Poet Laureate of the Tay Bridge'. He meant his poetry to be taken seriously, but it sits firmly in the realms of doggerel and his style has always raised a smile.

His beloved bridge carried Ulysses S. Grant, the Emperor of Brazil and Queen Victoria, who noted in her diary '. . . began going over the marvellous Tay Bridge, which is more than a mile and a half long . . . It took us, I should say about eight minutes going over. The view was very fine.'

Sadly the bridge only lasted another four months, a gale bringing disaster to both bridge and a train crossing at the time. McGonagall, unsurprisingly, wrote a poem about the disaster.

23

THE RAILWAY BRIDGE OF THE
SILVERY TAY

Beautiful Railway bridge of the Silvery Tay!
With your numerous arches and pillars in so grand array,
And your central girders, which seem to the eye
To be almost towering to the sky.
The greatest wonder of the day,
And a great beautification to the River Tay,
Most beautiful to be seen,
Near by Dundee and the Magdalen Green.

Beautiful Railway Bridge of the Silvery Tay!
That has caused the Emperor of Brazil to leave
His home far away, *incognito* in his dress,
And view thee ere he passed along *en route* to Inverness.

Beautiful Railway Bridge of the Silvery Tay!
The longest of the present day
That has ever crossed o'er a tidal river stream,
Most gigantic to be seen,
Near by Dundee and the Magdalen Green.

Beautiful Railway Bridge of the Silvery Tay!
Which will cause great rejoicing on the opening day,
And hundreds of people will come from far away,
Also the Queen, most gorgeous to be seen,
Near by Dundee and the Magdalen Green.

Beautiful Railway Bridge of the Silvery Tay!
And prosperity to Provost Cox, who has given
Thirty thousand pounds and upwards away
In helping to erect the Bridge of the Tay,
Most handsome to be seen,
Near by Dundee and the Magdalen Green.

Beautiful Railway Bridge of the Silvery Tay!
I hope that God will protect all passengers
By night and by day,
And that no accident will befall them while crossing
The Bridge of the Silvery Tay,
For that would be most awful to be seen
Near by Dundee and the Magdalen Green.

Beautiful Railway Bridge of the Silvery Tay!
And prosperity to Messrs Bouche and Grothe,
The famous engineers of the present day,
Who have succeeded in erecting the Railway
Bridge of the Silvery Tay,
Which stands unequalled to be seen
Near by Dundee and the Magdalen Green.

MARRIOTT EDGAR
1880–1951

———— ∞∞∞ ————

Marriott Edgar was a Scot who wrote monologues for the entertainer Stanley Holloway. Edgar travelled round Britain with Holloway so that he could write topical material for Holloway to weave into his stage shows and seaside concert parties.

In 1932, Holloway and Edgar spotted a newspaper item about a child being attacked by a lion at London Zoo. Edgar set out to write a poem to mark the event for Holloway to perform, changing the location to Blackpool Zoo because he thought that would be funnier. When *The Lion and Albert* was finished, Holloway was uncertain how it would be received, so it was first performed at the Northern Rugby League Annual Dinner and Dance in Newcastle where it was a huge success. From then on *The Lion and Albert* became one of Holloway's 'standards' – wherever he performed.

24

THE LION AND ALBERT

There's a famous seaside place called Blackpool,
    That's noted for fresh air and fun,
And Mr and Mrs Ramsbottom
    Went there with young Albert, their son.

A grand little lad was young Albert,
    All dressed in his best; quite a swell
With a stick with an 'orse's 'ead 'andle,
    The finest that Woolworth's could sell.

They didn't think much to the Ocean:
    The waves, they was fiddlin' and small,
There was no wrecks and nobody drownded,
    Fact, nothing to laugh at at all.

So, seeking for further amusement,
    They paid and went into the Zoo,
Where they'd Lions and Tigers and Camels,
    And old ale and sandwiches too.

There were one great big Lion called Wallace;
    His nose were all covered with scars—
He lay in a somnolent posture
    With the side of his face on the bars.

Now Albert had heard about Lions,
   How they was ferocious and wild—
To see Wallace lying so peaceful,
   Well, it didn't seem right to the child.

So straightway the brave little feller,
   Not showing a morsel of fear,
Took his stick with its 'orse's 'ead 'andle
   And poked it in Wallace's ear.

You could see that the Lion didn't like it,
   For giving a kind of a roll,
He pulled Albert inside the cage with 'im,
   And swallowed the little lad 'ole.

Then Pa, who had seen the occurrence,
   And didn't know what to do next,
Said 'Mother! Yon Lion's 'et Albert,'
   And Mother said 'Well, I am vexed!'

Then Mr and Mrs Ramsbottom—
   Quite rightly, when all's said and done—
Complained to the Animal Keeper
   That the Lion had eaten their son.

The keeper was quite nice about it;
   He said 'What a nasty mishap.
Are you sure that it's *your* boy he's eaten?'
   Pa said 'Am I sure? There's his cap!'

The manager had to be sent for.
    He came and he said 'What's to do?'
Pa said 'Yon Lion's 'et Albert,
    And 'im in his Sunday clothes, too.'

Then Mother said, 'Right's right, young feller;
    I think it's a shame and a sin
For a lion to go and eat Albert,
    And after we've paid to come in.'

The manager wanted no trouble,
    He took out his purse right away,
Saying 'How much to settle the matter?'
    And Pa said 'What do you usually pay?'

But Mother had turned a bit awkward
    When she thought where her Albert had gone.
She said 'No! someone's got to be summonsed'—
    So that was decided upon.

Then off they went to the P'lice Station,
    In front of the Magistrate chap;
They told 'im what happened to Albert,
    And proved it by showing his cap.

The Magistrate gave his opinion
    That no one was really to blame
And he said that he hoped the Ramsbottoms
    Would have further sons to their name.

At that Mother got proper blazing,
  'And thank you, sir, kindly,' said she.
'What, waste all our lives raising children
  To feed ruddy Lions? Not me!'

A Subaltern's Love-song – John Betjeman

'A Subaltern's Love-song' was inspired by Joan Hunter Dunn, a young girl from Aldershot who was working at the Ministry of Information at the same time as Betjeman. He wrote the poem as an imaginary scenario. A few years later, in 1945, the Betjemans were invited to her wedding, but they were unable to attend.

25

A SUBALTERN'S LOVE-SONG

Miss J. Hunter Dunn, Miss J. Hunter Dunn,
Furnish'd and burnish'd by Aldershot sun,
What strenuous singles we played after tea,
We in the tournament – you against me!

Love-thirty, love-forty, oh! weakness of joy,
The speed of a swallow, the grace of a boy,
With carefullest carelessness, gaily you won,
I am weak from your loveliness, Joan Hunter Dunn.

Miss Joan Hunter Dunn, Miss Joan Hunter Dunn,
How mad I am, sad I am, glad that you won.
The warm-handled racket is back in its press,
But my shock-headed victor, she loves me no less.

Her father's euonymus shines as we walk,
And swing past the summer-house, buried in talk,
And cool the verandah that welcomes us in
To the six-o'clock news and a lime-juice and gin.

The scent of the conifers, sound of the bath,
The view from my bedroom of moss-dappled path,
As I struggle with double-end evening tie,
For we dance at the Golf Club, my victor and I.

On the floor of her bedroom lie blazer and shorts
And the cream-coloured walls are be-trophied with sports,
And westering, questioning settles the sun
On your low-leaded window, Miss Joan Hunter Dunn.

The Hillman is waiting, the light's in the hall,
The pictures of Egypt are bright on the wall,
My sweet, I am standing beside the oak stair
And there on the landing the light's on your hair.

By roads 'not adopted', by woodlanded ways,
She drove to the club in the late summer haze,
Into nine-o'clock Camberley, heavy with bells
And mushroomy, pine-woody, evergreen smells.

Miss Joan Hunter Dunn, Miss Joan Hunter Dunn,
I can hear from the car-park the dance has begun.
Oh! full Surrey twilight! importunate band!
Oh! strongly adorable tennis-girl's hand!

Around us are Rovers and Austins afar,
Above us, the intimate roof of the car,
And here on my right is the girl of my choice,
With the tilt of her nose and the chime of her voice,

And the scent of her wrap, and the words never said,
And the ominous, ominous dancing ahead.
We sat in the car-park till twenty to one
And now I'm engaged to Miss Joan Hunter Dunn.

OGDEN NASH
1902–71

———— ∞∞∞ ————

Frederic Ogden Nash was born in Rye, New York, in 1902, the great-great-great-nephew of General Francis Nash, after whom Nashville is named.

Nash attended Harvard briefly from 1920–21 before deciding to go out into the world to earn a living. He worked first as a teacher and then a copywriter before switching to publishing.

He worked on the editorial staff of the *New Yorker* and in 1925 saw his first book, *The Cricket of Carador*, published. This book for children was co-written with Joseph Alger. Six years later came Nash's first book of humorous verse, *Hard Lines*. In his writings he successfully twisted and misspelled words in order to manufacture rhymes. Nash always said he had been influenced by Julia Moore (America's William McGonagall). He became a much-loved figure in the States through his silly, often cynical poems of observation, always in demand for TV and radio shows during the 1940s and 1950s. With Kurt Weill and S. J. Perelman he wrote the 1943 Broadway hit musical *One Touch of Venus*.

26

THE TALE OF CUSTARD THE DRAGON

Belinda lived in a little white house,
With a little black kitten and a little gray mouse,
And a little yellow dog and a little red wagon,
And a realio, trulio, little pet dragon.

Now the name of the little black kitten was Ink,
And the little gray mouse, she called her Blink,
And the little yellow dog, as sharp as Mustard,
But the dragon was a coward, and she called him Custard.

Custard the dragon had big sharp teeth,
And spikes on top of him and scales underneath,
Mouth like a fireplace, chimney for a nose,
And realio, trulio daggers on his toes.

Belinda was as brave as a barrel full of bears,
And Ink and Blink chased lions down the stairs,
Mustard was as brave as a tiger in a rage,
But Custard cried for a nice safe cage.

Belinda tickled him, she tickled him unmerciful,
Ink, Blink and Mustard, they rudely called him Percival,
They all sat laughing in the little red wagon
At the realio, trulio, cowardly dragon.

Belinda giggled till she shook the house,
And Blink said Weeck! which is giggling for a mouse,
Ink and Mustard rudely asked his age,
When Custard cried for a nice safe cage.

Suddenly, suddenly they heard a nasty sound,
And Mustard growled, and they all looked around.
Meowch! cried Ink, and Ooh! cried Belinda,
For there was a pirate, climbing in the winda.

Pistol in his left hand, pistol in his right,
And he held in his teeth a cutlass bright,
His beard was black, one leg was wood;
It was clear that the pirate meant no good.

Belinda paled, and she cried Help! Help!
But Mustard fled with a terrified yelp,
Ink trickled down to the bottom of the household,
And little mouse Blink strategically mouseholed.

But up jumped Custard, snorting like an engine,
Clashed his tail like irons in a dungeon
With a clatter and a clank and a jangling squirm
He went at the pirate like a robin at a worm.

The pirate gaped at Belinda's dragon,
And gulped some grog from his pocket flagon,
He fired two bullets, but they didn't hit,
And Custard gobbled him, every bit.

Belinda embraced him, Mustard licked him,
No one mourned for his pirate victim.
Ink and Blink in glee did gyrate
Around the dragon that ate the pyrate.

Belinda still lives in her little white house,
With her little black kitten and her little gray mouse,
And her little yellow dog and her little red wagon,
And her realio, trulio, little pet dragon.

Belinda is as brave as a barrel full of bears,
And Ink and Blink chase lions down the stairs.
Mustard is as brave as a tiger in a rage,
But Custard keeps crying for a nice safe cage.

A. A. MILNE
1882–1956

Alan Alexander Milne was born in London in 1882 and educated at Westminster School and Trinity College, Cambridge. In 1903 he went into journalism and three years later had risen to assistant editor of *Punch*. He began to pen plays during the First World War while writing propaganda for the Intelligence Service, and by the end of the conflict had become sufficiently proficient to go into freelance writing. Between 1924 and 1928 he wrote the children's books that established him as a writer: *When We Were Very Young*, *A Gallery of Children*, *The King's Breakfast*, *Winnie-the-Pooh*, *Now We Are Six* and *The House at Pooh Corner*. The thirty or so plays he wrote between 1918 and 1951 have mostly faded from memory now, except his stage adaptation of Kenneth Grahame's *The Wind in the Willows*, *Toad of Toad Hall*.

Milne and his wife Dorothy de Selincourt, whom he married in 1931, had one son, Christopher Robin, who was portrayed in the writer's children's books, including *Winnie-the-Pooh*.

The Pooh books are set near Milne's country home, at the edge of the Ashdown Forest in Sussex.

The King's Breakfast – A. A. Milne

'The King's Breakfast' featured alongside other classic Milne poems 'Vespers' and 'Buckingham Palace' in his 1924 publication *When We Were Very Young*. Those three poems and many others have since been set very successfully to music. 'The King's Breakfast' was later published with 'decorations' by E. H. Shepard, the artist who worked in tandem with Milne and produced the famous drawings of Winnie-the-Pooh and his friends.

$\boxed{27}$

THE KING'S BREAKFAST

The King asked
The Queen, and
The Queen asked
The Dairymaid:
'Could we have some butter for
The Royal slice of bread?'
The Queen asked
The Dairymaid,
The Dairymaid
Said: 'Certainly,
I'll go and tell
The cow
Now
Before she goes to bed.'

The Dairymaid
She curtsied,
And went and told
The Alderney:
'Don't forget the butter for
The Royal slice of bread.'
The Alderney
Said sleepily:
'You'd better tell
His Majesty
That many people nowadays

Like marmalade
Instead.'

The Dairymaid
Said: 'Fancy!'
And went to
Her Majesty.
She curtsied to the Queen, and
She turned a little red:
'Excuse me,
Your Majesty,
For taking of
The liberty,
But marmalade is tasty, if
It's very
Thickly
Spread.'

The Queen said:
'Oh!'
And went to
His Majesty:
'Talking of the butter for
The Royal slice of bread,
Many people
Think that
Marmalade
Is nicer.
Would you like to try a little
Marmalade
Instead?'

The King said:
'Bother!'
And then he said:
'Oh, deary me!'
The King sobbed: 'Oh, deary me!'
And went back to bed.
'Nobody,'
He whimpered,
'Could call me
A fussy man;
I *only* want
A little bit
Of butter for
My bread!'

The Queen said:
'There, there!'
And went to
The Dairymaid.
The Dairymaid
Said: 'There, there!'
And went to the shed.
The cow said:
'There, there!
I didn't really
Mean it;
Here's milk for his porringer
And butter for his bread.'

The Queen took
The butter
And brought it to
His Majesty;
The King said:
'Butter, eh?'
And bounced out of bed.
'Nobody,' he said:
As he kissed her
Tenderly,
'Nobody,' he said,
As he slid down
The banisters,
'Nobody,
My darling,
Could call me
A fussy man—
BUT
I do like a little bit of butter to my bread!'

W. S. GILBERT
1836–1911

━━━━━ ∞ ━━━━━

William Schwenk Gilbert was born in 1836 and educated at King's College, London. After four years as a clerk at the Privy Council Office he left to study law. For several years he was a practising, but unsuccessful, barrister, and in 1861 he began to contribute comic verse to a magazine called *Fun*.

These verses were collected and published in 1869 as the *Bab Ballads*. Some of this formed the basis of light stage works which he began to create, but his finest hour was yet to come. In 1869 he met the composer Arthur Sullivan, and the impresario D'Oyly Carte five years later. D'Oyly Carte leased the Opéra Comique to stage Gilbert and Sullivan's operas, building the Savoy Theatre in 1881 specially for the D'Oyly Carte Company. It was here that Gilbert and Sullivan's finest light operas were staged, including *Patience*, *HMS Pinafore*, *The Pirates of Penzance*, *The Mikado*, *The Yeoman of the Guard* and *Iolanthe*.

After 1896 Gilbert continued to write plays and operas without Sullivan, including *Rosencrantz and Guildenstern*. He used his profits to build the Garrick Theatre, and was knighted in 1907. He died in 1911 while attempting to rescue a girl who'd fallen into a lake.

The Nightmare – W. S. Gilbert

'The Nightmare' comes from a song featured in W. S. Gilbert's fairy opera *Iolanthe* (or *The Peer and the Peri*), with music by Arthur Sullivan. It was first performed at the Savoy Theatre, London, on 25 November 1882, when George Grossmith played the role of the Lord Chancellor. It's this character who sings 'The Nightmare' in Act Two, when his love for an Arcadian shepherdess, Phyllis, is giving him nightmares.

The object of the Lord Chancellor's (and most other men's) desires, Phyllis was played by Leonora Braham in the original production. Sullivan's music suggests the tempo should be *allegro ma non troppo* . . . just in case you should intend to read it at the intended pace!

28

THE NIGHTMARE

When you're lying awake with a dismal headache, and
   repose is taboo'd by anxiety,
I conceive you may use any language you choose to
   indulge in, without impropriety;
For your brain is on fire – the bedclothes conspire of
   usual slumber to plunder you:
First your counterpane goes, and uncovers your toes, and
   your sheet slips demurely from under you;
Then the blanketing tickles – you feel like mixed pickles
   – so terribly sharp is the pricking,
And you're hot, and you're cross, and you tumble and
   toss till there's nothing 'twixt you and the ticking.
Then the bedclothes all creep to the ground in a heap,
   and you pick 'em all up in a tangle;
Next your pillow resigns and politely declines to remain
   at its usual angle!
Well, you get some repose in the form of a doze, with
   hot eye-balls and head ever aching,
But your slumbering teems with such horrible dreams
   that you'd very much better be waking;
For you dream you are crossing the Channel, and toss-
   ing about in a steamer from Harwich—
Which is something between a large bathing machine
   and a very small second-class carriage—

And you're giving a treat (penny ice and cold meat) to a
    party of friends and relations—
They're a ravenous horde – and they all came on board
    at Sloane Square and South Kensington Stations.
And bound on that journey you find your attorney (who
    started that morning from Devon);
He's a bit undersized, and you don't feel surprised when
    he tells you he's only eleven.
Well, you're driving like mad with this singular lad
    (by-the-by the ship's now a four-wheeler),
And you're playing round games, and he calls you bad
    names when you tell him that 'ties pay the dealer';
But this you can't stand, so you throw up your hand, and
    you find you're as cold as an icicle,
In your shirt and your socks (the black silk with gold
    clocks), crossing Salisbury Plain on a bicycle:
And he and the crew are on bicycles too – which they've
    somehow or other invested in—
And he's telling the tars, all the particu*lars* of a com-
    pany he's interested in—
It's a scheme of devices, to get at low prices, all goods
    from cough mixtures to cables
(Which tickled the sailors) by treating retailers, as though
    they were all vege*t*ables—
You get a good spadesman to plant a small tradesman,
    (first take off his boots with a boot-tree),
And his legs will take root, and his fingers will shoot,
    and they'll blossom and bud like a fruit-tree—

From the greengrocer tree you get grapes and green pea,
    cauliflower, pineapple, and cranberries,
While the pastrycook plant, cherry brandy will grant,
    apple puffs, and three-corners, and banberries—
The shares are a penny, and ever so many are taken by
    Rothschild and Baring,
And just as a few are allotted to you, you awake with a
    shudder despairing—
You're a regular wreck, with a crick in your neck, and
    no wonder you snore, for your head's on the floor, and
    you've needles and pins from your soles to your shins,
    and your flesh is a-creep for your left leg's asleep, and
    you've cramp in your toes, and a fly on your nose, and
    some fluff in your lung, and a feverish tongue, and a thirst
    that's intense, and a general sense that you haven't been
    sleeping in clover;
But the darkness has passed, and it's daylight at last, and
    the night has been long – ditto ditto my song – and thank
    goodness they're both of them over!

Hiawatha's Photographing – Lewis Carroll

Lewis Carroll had first become keen on photography, a new craze sweeping the country in the 1850s, by watching his Uncle Skeffington Lutwidge at work with his camera. The flames of enthusiasm were fanned further following a visit to the Photographic Society annual exhibition in London in 1865. For £15 he bought a camera from T. Ottewill of Charlotte Street, Caledonia Road, London, and embarked on a pastime that would lead to him photographing many famous people, including Holman Hunt, Tennyson, Sir John Millais, John Ruskin, Faraday, Ellen Terry, Dante Gabriel and Christina Rossetti, and the Duke of Albany.

It was the misreading of his photographing of young girls and the suggestion of some nude photography that led to his abandoning his camera in 1880. In this poem, his interest in the art is demonstrated within the framework of the easily, and often parodied, 'Hiawatha' by Longfellow.

29

HIAWATHA'S PHOTOGRAPHING

From his shoulder Hiawatha
Took the camera of rosewood—
Made of sliding, folding rosewood—
Neatly put it all together.
   In its case it lay compactly,
Folded into nearly nothing;
But he opened out its hinges,
Pushed and pulled the joints and hinges
Till it looked all squares and oblongs,
Like a complicated figure
In the second book of Euclid.
   This he perched upon a tripod,
And the family, in order
Sat before him for their pictures—
Mystic, awful, was the process.
   First, a piece of glass he coated
With collodion, and plunged it
In a bath of lunar caustic
Carefully dissolved in water—
There he left it certain minutes.
   Secondly, my Hiawatha
Made with cunning hand a mixture
Of the acid pyrro-gallic,
And of glacial-acetic,
And of alcohol and water—

This developed all the picture.
  Finally, he fixed each picture
With a saturate solution
Which was made of hyposulphite
Which, again, was made of soda.
(Very difficult the name is
For a metre like the present
But periphrasis has done it.)
  All the family, in order,
Sat before him for their pictures;
Each in turn, as he was taken,
Volunteered his own suggestions—
His invaluable suggestions.
  First, the governor – the father—
He suggested velvet curtains
Looped about a massy pillar,
And the corner of a table—
Of a rosewood dining table.
He would hold a scroll of something—
Hold it firmly in his left hand;
He would keep his right hand buried
(Like Napoleon) in his waistcoat;
He would gaze upon the distance—
(Like a poet seeing visions,
Like a man that plots a poem,
In a dressing gown of damask,
At 12.30 in the morning,
Ere the servants bring in luncheon)—
With a look of pensive meaning,
As of ducks that die in tempests.

Grand, heroic was the notion:
Yet the picture failed entirely,
Failed because he moved a little—
Moved because he couldn't help it.
    Next his better half took courage—
She would have her picture taken:
She came dressed beyond description,
Dressed in jewels and in satin,
Far too gorgeous for an empress.
Gracefully she sat down sideways,
With a simper scarcely human,
Holding in her hand a nosegay
Rather larger than a cabbage.
    All the while that she was taking,
Still the lady chattered, chattered,
Like a monkey in the forest.
'Am I sitting still?' she asked him;
'Is my face enough in profile?
Shall I hold the nosegay higher?
Will it come into the picture?'
And the picture failed completely.
    Next the son, the stunning Cantab—
He suggested curves of beauty,
Curves pervading all his figure,
Which the eye might follow onward
Till it centred in the breast-pin—
Centred in the golden breast-pin.
He had learnt it all from Ruskin,
(Author of *The Stones of Venice*,
Seven Lamps of Architecture,

Modern Painters, and some others)—
And perhaps he had not fully
Understood the author's meaning;
But, whatever was the reason,
All was fruitless, as the picture
Ended in a total failure.

    After him the eldest daughter:
She suggested very little,
Only begged she might be taken
With her look of 'passive beauty'.
Her idea of passive beauty
Was a squinting of the left eye,
Was a drooping of the right eye,
Was a smile that went up sideways
To the corner of the nostrils.

    Hiawatha, when she asked him,
Took no notice of the question,
Looked as if he hadn't heard it;
But, when pointedly appealed to,
Smiled in a peculiar manner,
Coughed, and said it 'didn't matter',
Bit his lips, and changed the subject.

    Nor in this was he mistaken,
As the picture failed completely.

    So, in turn, the other daughters:
All of them agreed on one thing,
That their pictures came to nothing,
Though they differed in their causes,
From the eldest, Grinny-haha,
Who, throughout her time of taking,

Shook with sudden, ceaseless laughter,
With a silent fit of laughter,
To the youngest, Dinny-wawa,
Shook with sudden, causeless weeping—
Anything but silent weeping:
And their pictures failed completely.
Last, the youngest son was taken:
'John' his Christian name had once been;
But his overbearing sisters
Called him names he disapproved of—
Called him Johnny, 'Daddy's Darling'—
Called him Jacky, 'Scrubby Schoolboy'.
Very rough and thick his hair was,
Very dusty was his jacket,
Very fidgetty his manner,
And, so fearful was the picture,
In comparison the others
Might be thought to have succeeded—
To have partially succeeded.
    Finally, my Hiawatha
Tumbled all the tribe together
('Grouped' is not the right expression),
And, as happy chance would have it,
Did at last obtain a picture
Where the faces all succeeded:
Each came out a perfect likeness.
    Then they joined and all abused it—
Unrestrainedly abused it—
As 'the worst and ugliest picture
That could possibly be taken

Giving one such strange expressions!
Sulkiness, conceit, and meanness!
Really any one would take us
(Any one who did not know us)
For the most unpleasant people!'
(Hiawatha seemed to think so—
Seemed to think it not unlikely).
All together rang their voices—
Angry, hard, discordant voices—
As of dogs that howl in concert,
As of cats that wail in chorus.
  But my Hiawatha's patience,
His politeness and his patience,
Unaccountably had vanished,
And he left that happy party.
Neither did he leave them slowly,
With the calm deliberation,
The intense deliberation
Of a photographic artist:
But he left them in a hurry,
Left them in a mighty hurry,
Stating that he would not stand it,
Stating in emphatic language
What he'd be before he'd stand it.
Hurriedly he packed his boxes:
Hurriedly the porter trundled
On a barrow all his boxes:
Hurriedly he took his ticket:
Hurriedly the train received him:
Thus departed Hiawatha.

ALAN AHLBERG
born 1938

———— ∞∞∞ ————

Born in 1938, and educated in Sunderland, Ahlberg has been a postman, soldier, teacher, grave-digger and plumber's mate. His writing for children has won him many awards, and his collaboration with his late wife Janet, who was a wonderful illustrator, resulted in many outstanding books being published in many languages throughout the world. He lives in Burstall, Leicestershire.

30

PLEASE MRS BUTLER

Please Mrs Butler
This boy Derek Drew
Keeps copying my work, Miss.
What shall I do?

Go and sit in the hall, dear.
Go and sit in the sink.
Take your books on the roof, my lamb.
Do whatever you think.

Please Mrs Butler
This boy Derek Drew
Keeps taking my rubber, Miss.
What shall I do?

Keep it in your hand, dear.
Hide it up your vest.
Swallow it if you like, my love.
Do what you think best.

Please Mrs Butler
This boy Derek Drew
Keeps calling me rude names, Miss.
What shall I do?

Lock yourself in the cupboard, dear.
Run away to sea.
Do whatever you can, my flower.
But *don't ask me!*

E. V. KNOX
1881–1971

———❦———

Born Edmund George Valpy Knox in 1881, he was
known as 'Evoe' and was the brother of the Rt Revd
Monsignor Ronald Arbuthnott Knox (1888–1957), whose
biography was written by Evelyn Waugh. 'Evoe' was a
humorist as well as a writer of essays and parodies. He
contributed to *Punch* as 'Evoe' before becoming its editor
from 1932 to 1949.

31

THE EVERLASTING PERCY OR
MR MASEFIELD ON THE RAILWAY CENTENARY

I used to be a fearful lad,
The things I did were downright bad;
And worst of all were what I done
From seventeen to twenty-one
On all the railways far and wide
From sinfulness and shameful pride.

For several years I was so wicked
I used to go without a ticket,
And travelled underneath the seat
Down in the dust of people's feet,
Or else I sat as bold as brass
And told them 'Season' in first class.
In 1921, at Harwich,
I smoked in a non-smoking carriage;
I never knew what Life nor Art meant,
I wrote 'Reserved' on my compartment,
And once (I was a guilty man)
I swapped the labels in guard's van.
From 1922 to 4
I leant against the carriage door
Without a-looking at the latch;
And once, a-leaving Colney Hatch,
I put a huge and heavy parcel

Which I were taking to Newcastle,
Entirely filled with lumps of lead,
Up on the rack above my head;
And when it tumbled down, oh Lord!
I pulled communication cord.
The guard came round and said, 'You mule!
What have you done, you dirty fool?'
I simply sat and smiled, and said
'Is this train right for Holyhead?'
He said 'You blinking blasted swine,
You'll have to pay the five-pound fine.'
I gave a false name and address,
Puffed up with my vaingloriousness.
At Bickershaw and Strood and Staines
I've often got on moving trains,
And once alit at Norwood West
Before my coach had come to rest.
A window and a lamp I broke
At Chipping Sodbury and Stoke
And worse I did at Wissendine:
I threw out bottles on the line
And other articles as be
Likely to cause great injury
To persons working on the line—
That's what I did at Wissendine.
I grew so careless what I'd do
Throwing things out, and dangerous too,
That, last and worst of all I'd done,
I threw a great sultana bun
Out of the train at Pontypridd—

It hit a platelayer, it did.
I thought that I should have to swing
And never hear the sweet birds sing.
The jury recommended mercy,
And that's how grace was given to Percy.

And now I have a motor-bike
And up and down the road I hike,
Seeing the pretty birds and flowers,
And windmills with their sails and towers,
And all the wide sweep of the downs,
And villages and country towns,
And hear the mowers mowing hay,
And smell the great sea far away!
And always keeping – cars be blowed!—
Well on the wrong side of the road,
And never heeding hoots nor warners,
Especially around the corners,
For even down the steepest hill
Redemption saves me from a spill.

I have a flapper on my carrier
And some day I am going to marry her.

HILAIRE BELLOC

(see page 17 for biography)

(see page 17 for biography)

[32]

HENRY KING
WHO CHEWED BITS OF STRING, AND WAS EARLY CUT OFF IN DREADFUL AGONIES

The Chief Defect of Henry King
Was chewing little bits of String.
At last he swallowed some which tied
Itself in ugly Knots inside.
Physicians of the Utmost Fame
Were called at once; but when they came
They answered, as they took their Fees,
'There is no Cure for this Disease.
Henry will very soon be dead.'
His Parents stood about his Bed
Lamenting his Untimely Death,
When Henry, with his Latest Breath,
Cried 'Oh, my Friends, be warned by me,
That Breakfast, Dinner, Lunch, and Tea
Are all the Human Frame requires . . .'
With that, the Wretched Child expires.

W. M. PRAED
1802–1839

—◦◦◦—

Winthrop Mackintosh Praed was born in 1802 and educated at Eton, where he founded the school magazine, the *Etonian*. He went up to Trinity College, Oxford, was called to the Bar and then went into Parliament. Praed became Secretary to the Board of Control in 1834. Often compared to Hood, he was a writer of light verse, often disguising a darker subject with a lighter mood. Praed was a close friend of the writer Thomas Babington Macauley and was MP at various times for Calne, Leeds and Edinburgh. Praed died from consumption at the age of thirty-seven.

33

ARRIVALS AT A WATERING-PLACE

'I play a spade. – Such strange new faces
  Are flocking in from near and far;
Such frights! – (Miss Dobbs holds all the aces)—
  One can't imagine who they are:
The lodgings at enormous prices,—
  New donkeys, and another fly;
And Madame Bonbon out of ices,
  Although we're scarcely in July:
We're quite as sociable as any,
  But one old horse can scarcely crawl;
And really, where there are so many,
  We can't tell where we ought to call.

'Pray who has seen the odd old fellow
  Who took the Doctor's house last week?—
A pretty chariot, – livery yellow,
  Almost as yellow as his cheek;
A widower, sixty-five, and surly,
  And stiffer than a poplar-tree;
Drinks rum and water, gets up early
  To dip his carcass in the sea;
He's always in a monstrous hurry,
  And always talking of Bengal;
They say his cook makes noble curry;—
  I think, Louisa, we should call.

'And so Miss Jones, the mantua-maker,
   Has let her cottage on the hill!—
The drollest man, – a sugar-baker
   Last year imported from the till;
Prates of his *'orses* and his *'oney*,
   Is quite in love with fields and farms;
A horrid Vandal, – but his money
   Will buy a glorious coat of arms;
Old Clyster makes him take the waters;
   Some say he means to give a ball;
And after all, with thirteen daughters,
   I think, Sir Thomas, you might call.

'That poor young man! – I'm sure and certain
   Despair is making up his shroud;
He walks all night beneath the curtain
   Of the dim sky and murky cloud;
Draws landscapes – throws such mournful glances;
   Writes verses, – has such splendid eyes;
An ugly name, – but Laura fancies
   He's some great person in disguise!—
And since his dress is all the fashion,
   And since he's very dark and tall,
I think that out of pure compassion,
   I'll get Papa to go and call.

'So Lord St Ives is occupying
   The whole of Mr Ford's hotel!
Last Saturday his man was trying
   A little nag I want to sell.

He brought a lady in the carriage;
   Blue eyes, – eighteen, or thereabouts;—
Of course, you know, we *hope* it's marriage,
   But yet the *femme de chambre* doubts.
She looked so pensive when we met her,
   Poor thing! – and such a charming shawl!—
Well! till we understand it better,
   It's quite impossible to call!

'Old Mr Fund, the London Banker,
   Arrived to-day at Premium Court;
I would not, for the world, cast anchor
   In such a horrid dangerous port;
Such dust and rubbish, lath and plaster,—
   (Contractors play the meanest tricks)—
The roof's as crazy as its master,
   And he was born in fifty-six;
Stairs creaking – cracks in every landing,—
   The colonnade is sure to fall;
We shan't find post or pillar standing,
   Unless we make great haste to call.

'Who was that sweetest of sweet creatures
   Last Sunday in the Rector's seat?
The finest shape, – the loveliest features,—
   I never saw such tiny feet!
My brother, – (this is quite between us)
   Poor Arthur, – 'twas a sad affair;
Love at first sight! – she's quite a Venus,
   But then she's poorer far than fair;

And so my father and my mother
  Agreed it would not do at all;
And so, – I'm sorry for my brother!—
  It's settled that we're not to call.

'And there's an author, full of knowledge;
  And there's a captain on half-pay;
And there's a baronet from college,
  Who keeps a boy and rides a bay;
And sweet Sir Marcus from the Shannon,
  Fine specimen of brogue and bone;
And Doctor Calipee, the canon,
  Who weighs, I fancy, twenty stone:
A maiden lady is adorning
  The faded front of Lily Hall:—
Upon my word, the first fine morning,
  We'll make a round, my dear, and call.'

Alas! disturb not, maid and matron,
  The swallow in my humble thatch;
Your son may find a better patron,
  Your niece may meet a richer match:
I can't afford to give a dinner,
  I never was on Almack's list;
And, since I seldom rise a winner,
  I never like to play at whist:
Unknown to me the stocks are falling,
  Unwatched by me the glass may fall:
Let all the world pursue its calling,—
  I'm not at home if people call.

THOMAS HOOD
1799–1845

———∞∞∞———

Hood was born in London on 23 May 1799, the son of a bookseller. Sent to Dundee to convalesce after tuberculosis, he began to contribute to local newspapers and periodicals before returning to London to continue his career in journalism. Assistant editor of the *London Magazine* at only twenty-two, he moved in literary circles where he met Hazlitt, Charles Lamb and Thomas de Quincey. He quickly became famous for his satirical wit, which he put to good use in his editorship of *The Gem* and its comic annual. One of his admirers described him as 'the starry soul, that shines when all is dark!', and he was of sufficient reputation to be a serious contender for the post of Poet Laureate after Southey's death in 1843. Shortly before his own death on 3 May 1845 he published his poem 'The Bridge of Sighs', which Thackeray described as 'his Corunna, his Heights of Abraham' – a great victory achieved in his dying hour.

34

FAITHLESS NELLY GRAY

Ben Battle was a soldier bold,
   And used to war's alarms;
But a cannon-ball took off his legs,
   So he laid down his arms!

Now as they bore him off the field,
   Said he, 'Let others shoot,
For here I leave my second leg,
   And the Forty-second Foot!'

The army-surgeons made him limbs:
   Said he – 'They're only pegs:
But there's as wooden members quite
   As represent my legs!'

Now Ben he loved a pretty maid,
   Her name was Nelly Gray;
So he went to pay her his devours
   When he'd devoured his pay!

But when he called on Nelly Gray,
   She made him quite a scoff;
And when she saw his wooden legs
   Began to take them off!

'Oh, Nelly Gray! Oh, Nelly Gray!
   Is this your love so warm?
The love that loves a scarlet coat
   Should be more uniform!'

Said she, 'I loved a soldier once,
   For he was blithe and brave;
But I will never have a man
   With both legs in the grave!

'Before you had those timber toes,
   Your love I did allow,
But then, you know, you stand upon
   Another footing now!'

'Oh, Nelly Gray! Oh, Nelly Gray!
   For all your jeering speeches,
At duty's call, I left my legs
   In Badajos's *breaches*!'

'Why then,' said she, 'you've lost the feet
   Of legs in war's alarms,
And now you cannot wear your shoes
   Upon your feats of arms!'

'Oh, false and fickle Nelly Gray;
   I know why you refuse:—
Though I've no feet – some other man
   Is standing in my shoes!

'I wish I ne'er had seen your face;
    But, now, a long farewell!
For you will be my death – alas!
    You will not be my *Nell*!'

Now when he went from Nelly Gray,
    His heart so heavy got—
And life was such a burthen grown,
    It made him take a knot!

So round his melancholy neck,
    A rope he did entwine,
And, for his second time in life,
    Enlisted in the Line!

One end he tied around a beam,
    And then removed his pegs,
And, as his legs were off, – of course,
    He soon was off his legs!

And there he hung, till he was dead
    As any nail in town,—
For though distress had cut him up,
    It could not cut him down!

A dozen men sat on his corpse,
    To find out why he died—
And they buried Ben in four cross-roads,
    With a *stake* in his inside!

CHARLES CAUSLEY
born 1917

Born in Launceston, Cornwall, in 1917, Causley has lived there most of his life.

Educated at Horwell Grammar School and Launceston College, he began work in a series of office jobs in 1933. In his spare time he wrote poetry, stories and plays, finding some success with the latter when one of his works was performed on the radio in 1939. From 1940 to 1946 he served in the Navy, eventually rising to the rank of Petty Officer. Following the war he spent a year at Peterborough Training College, before returning to Launceston in 1947 and a job as a teacher, a profession he stayed in until 1976. In 1971 he received a Cholmondeley Award, and during 1973 and 1974 he was a Visiting Fellow in Poetry at Exeter University. Causley was awarded the CBE in 1986.

Betjeman 1984 – Charles Causley

Causley was admired by Betjeman to such an extent that when the latter was appointed Poet Laureate in October 1972, he wrote to Philip Larkin saying that *he* (Larkin) was the one who should have got the job, and failing him, Causley.

In 1981, Causley was one of twenty poets who contributed to a specially commissioned book of poems for Betjeman's seventy-fifth birthday. *A Garland for the Laureate* was presented to the Laureate and a limited edition of 350 copies was published.

In this poem, written in pure 'Betjeman', Causley includes references to Betjeman's close friends John and Myfanwy Piper, Pamela Mitford and the church of St Enodoc, where Betjeman is buried.

35

BETJEMAN, 1984

I saw him in the Airstrip Gardens
   (Fahrenheit at 451)
Feeding automative orchids
   With a little plastic bun,
While above his brickwork cranium
   Burned the trapped and troubled sun.

'Where is Piper? Where is Pontefract?
   (Devil take my boiling pate!)
Where is Pam? and where's Myfanwy?
   Don't remind me of the date!
Can it be that I am *really*
   Knocking on for 78?

'In my splendid State Apartment
   Underneath a secret lock
Finger now forbidden treasures
   (Pray for me St Enodoc!):
TV plate and concrete lamp-post
   And a single nylon sock.

'Take your ease, pale-haired admirer,
   As I, half the century saner,
Pour a vintage Mazawattee
   Through the Marks and Spencer strainer
In a *genuine* British Railways
   (Luton Made) cardboard container.

'Though they say my verse-compulsion
    Lacks an interstellar drive,
Reading Beverley and Daphne
    Keeps *my* sense of words alive.
Lord, but *how* much beauty was there
    Back in 1955!'

W. H. AUDEN
1907–73

——— ∞∞∞ ———

Wystan Hugh Auden was born on 21 February 1907 in York, the third son of Dr G. A. Auden, who was inspired by memories of his schooldays when it came to choosing a name for the boy. Dr Auden had been a pupil at Repton in Derbyshire, and the nearby parish church is dedicated to St Wystan. At the age of eight, young Wystan was sent to St Edmund's School, Hindhead, Surrey; here he met Christopher Isherwood, who was to become a lifelong personal and literary friend.

Auden was already a published poet by the time he went up to Christ Church, Oxford, where his friends included John Betjeman, Cecil Day-Lewis, Louis MacNeice and Stephen Spender. Amongst his tutors was J. R. R. Tolkien, who inspired Auden with something of his own passion for Anglo-Saxon and Middle English poetry. During the 1930s Auden established himself as both a poet and a playwright, working at times in collaboration with Isherwood and with the composer Benjamin Britten, whom he met while attached to the GPO Film Unit. His move to America on the eve of war in 1939 was heavily criticised, and it took him some time to regain his former popularity. Nevertheless he was appointed Professor of Poetry at Oxford in 1956 and made a Fellow of Christ Church in 1962. He died at his house in Kirchstetten, Austria, on 29 September 1973.

36

THE UNKNOWN CITIZEN
(To JS/07/M/378
This Marble Monument Is Erected by the State)

He was found by the Bureau of Statistics to be
One against whom there was no official complaint,
And all the reports on his conduct agree
That, in the modern sense of an old-fashioned word, he
    was a saint,
For in everything he did he served the Greater
    Community.
Except for the War till the day he retired
He worked in a factory and never got fired,
But satisfied his employers, Fudge Motors Inc.
Yet he wasn't a scab or odd in his views,
For his Union reports that he paid his dues,
(Our report on his Union shows it was sound)
And our Social Psychology workers found
That he was popular with his mates and liked a drink.
The Press are convinced that he bought a paper every
    day
And that his reactions to advertisements were normal in
    every way.
Policies taken out in his name prove that he was fully
    insured,
And his Health-card shows he was once in hospital but
left it cured.

Both Producers Research and High-Grade Living declare
He was fully sensible to the advantages of the
   Instalment Plan
And had everything necessary to the Modern Man,
A phonograph, a radio, a car and a frigidaire.
Our researchers into Public Opinion are content
That he held the proper opinions for the time of year;
When there was peace, he was for peace; when there
   was war, he went.
He was married and added five children to the
   population,
Which our Eugenist says was the right number for a
   parent of his generation,
And our teachers report that he never interfered with
   their education.
Was he free? Was he happy? The question is absurd:
Had anything been wrong, we should certainly have
   heard.

NOËL COWARD
1899–1973

———— ∞∞∞ ————

Born in Teddington, Middlesex, in 1899, the son of a piano salesman, Coward was encouraged by his mother to go into the theatre. As a child actor he appeared in the 1913 production of *Peter Pan*, while his 1924 melodrama *The Vortex*, a play about drug addiction, was his fifth stage script as a playwright. It was with *Hay Fever* the following year that he really made his name.

He wrote dozens of highly successful songs, including 'Mad Dogs and Englishmen', 'I'll See You Again', 'Mad about the Boy', 'Let's Do It', and 'Room with a View', as well as acting in his own plays, the most notable being *Private Lives* with Gertrude Lawrence.

Other famous Coward plays included *Blithe Spirit*, *Cavalcade*, *Design for Living* and *Present Laughter*. Coward oozed glamour and sophistication in an era when it counted, but was slightly out of step by the 1960s when he looked down his nose at the Beatles. Coward died in 1973 but his plays and music are part of the theatrical fabric of the Nation.

During 1998 a tribute album was released featuring many major artists including Paul McCartney and Elton John performing Coward's songs.

There are Bad Times Just Around the Corner – Noël Coward

'There are Bad Times Just Around the Corner' stands up as a recital piece or a song and was first performed on stage in the Globe Revue of 1952 at London's Globe Theatre, with a cast that comprised George Benson, Dora Bryan, Ian Carmichael, Diana Decker, Joan Heal and Graham Payn.

37

THERE ARE BAD TIMES JUST AROUND THE CORNER

They're out of sorts in Sunderland,
They're terribly cross in Kent,
They're dull in Hull
And the Isle of Mull
Is seething with discontent;
They're nervous in Northumberland
And Devon is down the drain,
They're filled with wrath
In the Firth of Forth
And sullen on Salisbury Plain.
In Dublin they're depressed, lads,
Mainly because they're Celts,
For Drake is going West, lads,
And so is everyone else.
Hurray-hurray-hurray!
Misery's here to stay.

There are bad times just around the corner,
There are dark clouds hurtling through the sky,
And it's no good whining
About a silver lining
For we know from experience that they won't roll by.
With a scowl and frown
We'll keep our peckers down,

And prepare for depression and doom and dread,
We're going to unpack our troubles from our old kitbag
And wait until we drop down dead.

From Portland Bill to Scarborough
They're querulous and subdued
And Shropshire lads
Have behaved like cads
From Berwick-on-Tweed to Bude,
They're mad at Market Harborough
And livid at Leigh-on-Sea,
In Tunbridge Wells
You can hear the yells
Of woe-begone bourgeoisie.
We all get bitched about, lads,
Whoever our vote elects,
We know we're up the spout, lads,
And that's what England expects.
Hurray-hurray-hurray!
Trouble is on the way.

There are bad times just around the corner,
The horizon's gloomy as can be;
There are black birds over
The greyish cliffs of Dover,
And the rats are preparing to leave the BBC.
We're an unhappy breed
And very bored indeed
When reminded of something that Nelson said,
And while the press and the politicians nag nag nag
We'll wait until we drop down dead.

Coward

From Colwyn Bay to Kettering
They're sobbing themselves to sleep;
The shrieks and wails
In the Yorkshire dales
Have even depressed the sheep.
In rather vulgar lettering,
A very disgruntled group
Have posted bills
In the Cotswold Hills
To prove that we're in the soup.
While begging Kipling's pardon,
There's one thing we know for sure:
If England is a garden
We ought to have more manure.
Hurray-hurray-hurray!
Suffering and dismay.

There are bad times just around the corner,
And the outlook's absolutely vile;
There are Home Fires smoking
From Windermere to Woking,
And we're *not* going to tighten our belts and smile
    smile smile.
At the sound of a shot
We'd just as soon as not
Take a hot-water bottle and go to bed:
We're going to *un*tense our muscles till they sag sag sag
And wait until we drop down dead.

There are bad times just around the corner,
We can all look forward to despair,
It's as clear as crystal
From Bridlington to Bristol
That we can't save democracy and we don't much care.
If the Reds and Pinks
Believe that England stinks,
And that world revolution is bound to spread,
We'd better all learn the lyrics of the old 'Red Flag'
And wait until we drop down dead—
A likely story,
Land of Hope and Glory,
Wait until we drop down dead.

HILAIRE BELLOC

(see page 17 for biography)

38

REBECCA,
WHO SLAMMED DOORS FOR FUN
AND PERISHED MISERABLY

A trick that everyone abhors
In Little Girls is slamming Doors,
A Wealthy Banker's Little Daughter
Who lived in Palace Green, Bayswater
(By name Rebecca Offendort),
Was given to this Furious Sport.

She would deliberately go
And Slam the door like Billy-Ho!
To make her Uncle Jacob start.
She was not really bad at heart,
But only rather rude and wild:
She was an aggravating child . . .

It happened that a Marble Bust
Of Abraham was standing just
Above the Door this little Lamb
Had carefully prepared to Slam,
And Down it came! It knocked her flat!
It laid her out! She looked like that.

Her funeral Sermon (which was long
And followed by a Sacred Song)
Mentioned her Virtues, it is true,
But dwelt upon her Vices too,
And showed the Dreadful End of One
Who goes and slams the door for Fun.

The children who were brought to hear
The awful Tale from far and near
Were much impressed, and inly swore
They never more would slam the Door.
—As often they had done before.

A. D. GODLEY
1856–1925

———— ⊗⊗⊗ ————

Born in 1856, Alfred Denis Godley became a classical scholar and public orator at Oxford. Joint editor of the *Classical Review*, he also wrote light verse, some of which incorporated his knowledge of Latin, as in 'The Motor Bus'. His serious works include his translations of Horace's odes and Herodotus's works. His books of verse include *Verses to Order* (1892), *Lyra Frivola* (1899) and *Reliquiae* – a collection put together after his death.

The Motor Bus – A. D. Godley

Godley was in his forties when the motor car was introduced. As he slipped into his fifties and sixties, it must have become an increasing irritant on the streets of his beloved Oxford. If a mixture of French and English is 'Franglais', is this mixture of English and Latin 'Anglatine'?

39

THE MOTOR BUS

What is this that roareth thus?
Can it be a Motor Bus?
Yes, the smell and hideous hum
Indicant Motorem Bum!
Implet in the Corn and High
Terror me Motoris Bi:
Bo Motori clamitabo
Ne Motore caedar a Bo—
Dative be or Ablative
So thou only let us live:—
Whither shall thy victims flee?
Spare us, spare us, Motor Be!
Thus I sang; and still anigh
Came in hordes Motores Bi,
Et complebat omne forum
Copia Motorum Borum.
How shall wretches live like us
Cincti Bis Motoribus?
Domine, defende nos
Contra hos Motores Bos!

ROGER McGOUGH
born 1937

———— ∞∞∞ ————

Born in Liverpool in 1937, Roger McGough was educated at St Mary's College in Crosby by the Irish Christian Brothers, before going up to Hull University, where he came under the influence, to an extent, of the University Librarian, Philip Larkin.

McGough then trained as a teacher. He was drawn into the Liverpool artistic circle, becoming a member on and off for ten years of pop group The Scaffold. He wrote much of the material for the trio, which comprised McGough, John Gorman and Mike McGear (McCartney). They had several hits, their biggest being 'Thank You Very Much' and the number-one 'Lily The Pink'. His poems were first published in 1967, after which he and fellow Liverpudlians Adrian Henri and Brian Patten became inextricably linked as 'The Liverpool Poets'.

Roger McGough has proved one of Britain's most successful performers, lecturers and writers of verse. His many accolades include an OBE for services to poetry.

He has been described by the Poetry Society as 'A sort of unofficial Poet Laureate'.

At Lunchtime – Roger McGough

A non-driver, Roger McGough has spent a good percentage of his life on buses – observing, daydreaming and writing, invariably using them as a mobile office. Written in the late 1960s, 'At Lunchtime' is a parable of the time – a warning against the permissive society. The poem was published in Penguin Modern Poets 10: *The Mersey Sound*.

40

AT LUNCHTIME

When the bus stopped suddenly
to avoid damaging
a mother and child in the road,
the younglady in the green hat sitting opposite,
was thrown across me,
and not being one to miss an opportunity
i started to make love.

At first, she resisted,
saying that it was too early in the morning,
and too soon after breakfast,
and anyway, she found me repulsive.
But when i explained
that this being a nuclearage
the world was going to end at lunchtime,
she took off her green hat,
put her busticket into her pocket
and joined in the exercise.

The buspeople,
and there were many of them,
were shockedandsurprised,
and amusedandannoyed.
But when word got around
that the world was going to end at lunchtime,
they put their pride in their pockets

with their bustickets
and made love one with the other.
And even the busconductor,
feeling left out,
climbed into the cab,
and struck up some sort of relationship with the driver.

That night,
on the bus coming home,
we were all a little embarrassed.
Especially me and the younglady in the green hat.
And we all started to say
in different ways
how hasty and foolish we had been.
But then, always having been a bitofalad,
i stood up and said it was a pity
that the world didnt nearly end every lunchtime,
and that we could always pretend.
And then it happened . . .

Quick asa crash
we all changed partners,
and soon the bus was aquiver
with white, mothball bodies doing naughty things.

And the next day
And everyday
In everybus
In everystreet
In everytown
In everycountry

People pretended
that the world was coming to an end at lunchtime.
It still hasnt.
Although in a way it has.

EDWARD LEAR

(*see page 4 for biography*)

41

THE QUANGLE WANGLE'S HAT

I

On the top of the Crumpetty Tree
  The Quangle Wangle sat,
But his face you could not see,
  On account of his Beaver Hat.
For his Hat was a hundred and two feet wide,
With ribbons and bibbons on every side
And bells, and buttons, and loops, and lace,
So that nobody ever could see the face
    Of the Quangle Wangle Quee.

II

The Quangle Wangle said
  To himself on the Crumpetty Tree,—
'Jam; and jelly; and bread;
  'Are the best food for me!
'But the longer I live on this Crumpetty Tree
'The plainer than ever it seems to me
'That very few people come this way
'And that life on the whole is far from gay!'
    Said the Quangle Wangle Quee.

III

But there came to the Crumpetty Tree,
   Mr and Mrs Canary;
And they said, – 'Did you ever see
   'Any spot so charmingly airy?
'May we build a nest on your lovely Hat?
Mr Quangle Wangle, grant us that!
'O please let us come and build a nest
'Of whatever material suits you best,
    'Mr Quangle Wangle Quee!'

IV

And besides, to the Crumpetty Tree
   Came the Stork, the Duck, and the Owl;
The Snail, and the Bumble-Bee,
   The Frog, and the Fimble Fowl;
(The Fimble Fowl, with a Corkscrew leg;)
And all of them said, – We humbly beg,
'We may build our homes on your lovely Hat,—
'Mr Quangle Wangle, grant us that!
    'Mr Quangle Wangle Quee!'

V

And the Golden Grouse came there,
   And the Pobble who has no toes,—
And the small Olympian bear,—
   And the Dong with a luminous nose.
And the Blue Baboon, who played the flute,—
And the Orient Calf from the Land of Tute,—
And the Attery Squash, and the Bisky Bat,—
All came and built on the lovely Hat
    Of the Quangle Wangle Quee.

VI

And the Quangle Wangle said
   To himself on the Crumpetty Tree,—
'When all these creatures move
   'What a wonderful noise there'll be!'
And at night by the light of the Mulberry moon
They danced to the Flute of the Blue Baboon,
On the broad green leaves of the Crumpetty Tree,
And all were as happy as happy could be,
    With the Quangle Wangle Quee.

W. S. Gilbert – The Modern Major-General

'The Modern Major-General' comes from *The Pirates of Penzance* or *the Slave of Duty*, a comic opera by W. S. Gilbert with music by Arthur Sullivan. First staged at the Bijou Theatre, Paignton, on 30 December 1879, it was later performed at the Opéra Comique in London on 3 April 1880 with George Grossmith as Major-General Stanley. Four years later it was produced at the Savoy Theatre with a juvenile cast, before being revived there in 1888, 1900 and 1908. Major-General Stanley sings the song towards the end of Act One, when he arrives to thwart the pirates' intentions of marrying his daughters, by declaring untruthfully that he is an orphan. The pirates eventually discover the truth but are stopped from killing him when the police ask the pirates to yield in the name of Queen Victoria. Being decent chaps, they concede defeat. In the event it turns out they're all young noblemen just letting off a bit of steam. Inevitably they marry the Major-General's four daughters.

42

THE MODERN MAJOR-GENERAL

I am the very pattern of a modern Major-Gineral,
I've information vegetable, animal, and mineral;
I know the kings of England, and I quote the fights
　historical,
From Marathon to Waterloo, in order categorical;
I'm very well acquainted, too, with matters
　mathematical,
I understand equations, both the simple and quadratical;
About binomial theorem I'm teeming with a lot o' news,
With interesting facts about the square of the
　hypotenuse.
I'm very good at integral and differential calculus,
I know the scientific names of beings animalculous.
In short, in matters vegetable, animal, and mineral,
I am the very model of a modern Major-Gineral.

I know our mythic history – KING ARTHUR'S and SIR
　CARADOC'S,
I answer hard acrostics, I've a pretty taste for paradox;
I quote in elegiacs all the crimes of HELIOGABALUS,
In conics I can floor peculiarities parabolous.
I tell undoubted RAPHAELS from GERARD DOWS and
　ZOFFANIES,
I know the croaking chorus from the 'Frogs' of
　ARISTOPHANES;
Then I can hum a fugue, of which I've heard the music's
　din afore,

And whistle all the airs from that confounded nonsense
  'Pinafore.'
Then I can write a washing-bill in Babylonic cuneiform,
And tell you every detail of CARACTACUS'S uniform.
In short, in matters vegetable, animal, and mineral,
I am the very model of a modern Major-Gineral.

In fact, when I know what is meant by 'mamelon' and
  'ravelin,'
When I can tell at sight a Chassepôt rifle from a javelin,
When such affairs as *sorties* and surprises I'm more
  wary at,
And when I know precisely what is meant by
  Commissariat,
When I have learnt what progress has been made in
  modern gunnery,
When I know more of tactics than a novice in a
  nunnery,
In short, when I've a smattering of elementary strategy,
You'll say a better Major-Gine*ral* has never *sat* a gee—
For my military knowledge, though I'm plucky and
  adventury,
Has only been brought down to the beginning of the
  century.
But still in learning vegetable, animal, and mineral,
I am the very model of a modern Major-Gineral!

Mad Dogs and Englishmen – Noël Coward

'Mad Dogs and Englishmen' was featured in Coward's 1932 revue *Words and Music*, starring Doris Hare, Joyce Barbour, Romney Brent, John Mills, Norah Howard and Ivy St Helier, at London's Adelphi Theatre.

43

MAD DOGS AND ENGLISHMEN

In tropical climes there are certain times of day,
When all the citizens retire
To tear their clothes off and perspire.
It's one of those rules that the greatest fools obey,
Because the sun is much too sultry
And one must avoid its ultry-violet ray . . .
The natives grieve when the white men leave their huts,
Because they're obviously definitely nuts!

Mad dogs and Englishmen
Go out in the midday sun.
The Japanese don't care to,
The Chinese wouldn't dare to,
Hindoos and Argentines sleep firmly from twelve to
    one,
But Englishmen detest a
Siesta.
In the Philippines there are lovely screens
To protect you from the glare.
In the Malay States there are hats like plates
Which the Britishers won't wear.
At twelve noon
The natives swoon
And no further work is done,
But mad dogs and Englishmen
Go out in the midday sun.

Coward

It's such a surprise for the Eastern eyes to see,
That though the English are effete
They're quite impervious to heat.
When the white man rides every native hides in glee,
Because the simple creatures hope he
Will impale his solar topee on a tree. . . .
It seems such a shame when the English claim the earth
That they give rise to such hilarity and mirth.

Mad dogs and Englishmen
Go out in the midday sun.
The toughest Burmese bandit
Can never understand it.
In Rangoon the heat of noon
Is just what the natives shun.
They put their Scotch or rye down
And lie down.
In a jungle town
Where the sun beats down
To the rage of man and beast,
The English garb
Of the English sahib
Merely gets a bit more creased.
In Bangkok
At twelve o'clock
They foam at the mouth and run,
But mad dogs and Englishmen
Go out in the midday sun.

NIGEL FORDE

An actor, writer and composer, Forde is also a director of the Riding Lights Company. During the 1980s he became the resident poet on BBC Radio 4's *Midweek* programme. His book of verse, *Fluffy Dice*, was so well received in 1987 that he had a second one, *The Dust behind the Door*, published a year later.

In 1991 his book of poetry, *Teaching the Wind Plurals*, was published. Forde has written a critical anthology of G. K. Chesterton entitled *A Motley Wisdom*, and he won an Emmy for 'Moses', the first of the nine-part BBC 2 series *Testament*. The same programme was also nominated for a Grammy. *Sea Fret* on page 295 is a delightful parody of John Masefield's famous, and oft-quoted poem *Sea Fever*.

He lives with his family near York and is currently working on a film script, writing, more poetry and achieving increasing success with his one-man show *For Whom the Bird Sings*. All this, one feels, he would gladly trade to open for England in a Test Match. His telephone number is available to the England selectors upon request.

44

A DAY TO REMEMBER

The British love their heritage,
Their pomp and pageantry;
And nothing suits them better than
An anniversary—
An excuse for a toast and a flag on a pole,
Or a plaque, or to plant a tree.
Every day of the year belongs to a saint
Or a much more colourful sinner:
Someone died, or someone was born
King Alfred burnt the dinner,
Or something remarkable happened, or
The West Indies brought on a spinner.
But the dullest day in all the year
Is the nineteenth of February,
For nothing of note took place today
As far as I can see,
And it's time we did something about it
And gave it identity.
So – let's make it a day when we celebrate
The oddest and worst that has been—
Whatever you like that's not already
Kept its memory green
We'll think of and drink to every year
On dull old Feb. nineteen.
It's the day of St Aloysius Lepp,

Patron saint of hopeless cases
Who turned too fast from temptation
And was strangled in his braces;
The day they invented nappy-rash,
Earwax and empty spaces.
It's the day on which David Coleman made sense,
And Cannon and Ball told jokes;
The day they discovered that Milton Keynes
Was just an elaborate hoax;
It's National Scum and Tidemark day,
And, in 356 BC
Hats were invented; the first was worn
At twenty-five past three.
It's National Flag-day Flag-day today;
And comments about the weather
Were first passed in England on Feb. the nineteenth,
And the Scots invented heather.
The day of the first known incidence
Of musak in restaurants;
It's a day to rejoice because square things don't roll
And Frenchmen live in France.
The Greeks were invented, and Income Tax,
Barry Manilow sang in tune,
And someone invented fluffy dice
To hang in the family saloon.
It's the day they passed the law that says
Whichever queue you decide on
Will be the slowest moving;
And it's one that can be relied on.
On February the nineteenth

Latin became a dead language;
The Cabinet stayed intact all day;
BR used the first welded sandwich.
But how to commemorate such a great day?
Have a party? Or write an encomium?
Monks can stay in and celibate
Round the monastery harmonium;
I suggest we observe – at 11 o'clock—
Two minutes' pandemonium.

VERNON SCANNELL
born 1922

───── ∞∞∞ ─────

Born in Spilsbury, Lincolnshire, in 1922, his family led a peripatetic life before settling in Aylesbury, Buckinghamshire, where the young Vernon attended Queen's Park School. A keen boxer with a flair for English, he was forced to curb his enthusiasm for both as he joined the London Highlanders during the Second World War. He fought in Africa and Normandy before being cut down by machine-gun fire at Caen. Hospitalised for some time, he deserted after the war and spent two years on the run earning his living by boxing and teaching children. He was eventually caught, court-martialled and discharged. His poems began to get published, the first volume of his work, *Graves and Resurrections*, emerging in 1948. Whilst continuing to write poetry and the occasional novel, he made his living teaching in Surrey from 1955 to 1962 before becoming a freelance writer.

45

POPULAR MYTHOLOGIES

Not all these legends, I suppose,
Are total lies:
Thousands of Welshmen at a rugby match
Sometimes surprise
By singing more or less in tune;
Quite a lot
Of bullies may be cowards, though too many
Are not.
It would make sense to revise most saws
About the tall:
For instance I've found that the bigger they are
The harder *I* fall.
Everyone knows about the Scots
And their miserliness,
The way they repeatedly cry 'Hoots mon!'
Though I must confess
I have often been embarrassed by their largesse
And not one
In my hearing has ever said 'Hoots mon'.
Of course the Jews
Are very easy to pin down:
They amuse
With comic names like Izzy, Solly,
Benny, Moses,
And like the Scots they're very mean

And have big noses.
The trouble is you can't be sure
That people with small
Noses and names like Patrick, Sean,
Peter or Paul
Are always to be trusted in fiscal matters.
Not at all.
And what of the famous cockney wit?
You'd hear greater
Intelligence, humour and verbal flair
From an alligator
Than the average East End Londoner.
And suicides?
Those who talk about it never do it?
What of the brides
Of darkness, Sexton, Woolf and Plath?
And those others
Chatterton, Beddoes, Hemingway, Crane?
This band of brothers
All descanted on the mortal theme.
But why go on thus?
Easy, but waste of effort to fill
An omnibus.
Surprising though how people still
Swallow all this
Prejudiced stuff – not us, of course,
Oh no, not us.

ANONYMOUS

46

IF ALL THE WORLD WERE PAPER

If all the world were paper,
And all the sea were inke;
And all the trees were bread and cheese,
What should we do for drinke?

If all the world were sand 'o,
Oh, then what should we lack 'o;
If as they say there were no clay,
How should we make tobacco?

If all our vessels ran 'a,
If none but had a crack 'a;
If Spanish apes eat all the grapes,
What should we do for sack 'a?

If fryers had no bald pates,
Nor nuns had no dark cloysters,
If all the seas were beans and pease,
What should we do for oysters?

If there had been no projects,
Nor none that did great wrongs;
If fidlers shall turne players all,
What should we doe for songs?

If all things were eternall,
And nothing their end bringing;
If this should be, then, how should we
Here make an end of singing?

HILAIRE BELLOC

(see page 17 for biography)

47

JIM,

WHO RAN AWAY FROM HIS NURSE, AND WAS EATEN BY A LION.

There was a Boy whose name was Jim;
His Friends were very good to him.
They gave him Tea, and Cakes, and Jam,
And slices of delicious Ham,
And Chocolate with pink inside,
And little Tricycles to ride,
And read him Stories through and through,
And even took him to the Zoo—
But there it was the dreadful Fate
Befell him, which I now relate.

You know – at least you *ought* to know,
For I have often told you so—
That Children never are allowed
To leave their Nurses in a Crowd;
Now this was Jim's especial Foible,
He ran away when he was able,
And on this inauspicious day

He slipped his hand and ran away!
He hadn't gone a yard when – Bang!
With open Jaws, a Lion sprang,
And hungrily began to eat
The Boy: beginning at his feet.

Now just imagine how it feels
When first your toes and then your heels,
And then by gradual degrees,
Your shins and ankles, calves and knees,
Are slowly eaten, bit by bit.

No wonder Jim detested it!
No wonder that he shouted 'Hi!'
The Honest Keeper heard his cry,
Though very fat he almost ran
To help the little gentleman.
'Ponto!' he ordered as he came
(For Ponto was the Lion's name),
'Ponto!' he cried, with angry Frown.
'Let go, Sir! Down, Sir! Put it down!'

The Lion made a sudden Stop,
He let the Dainty Morsel drop,
And slunk reluctant to his Cage,
Snarling with Disappointed Rage
But when he bent him over Jim,
The Honest Keeper's Eyes were dim.
The Lion having reached his Head,
The Miserable Boy was dead!

When Nurse informed his Parents, they
Were more Concerned than I can say:—
His Mother, as She dried her eyes,
Said, 'Well – it gives me no surprise,
He would not do as he was told!'
His Father, who was self-controlled,
Bade all the children round attend
To James' miserable end,
And always keep a-hold of Nurse
For fear of finding something worse.

THOMAS HOOD

(see page 131 for biography)

48

NO!

No sun – no moon!
No morn – no noon—
No dawn – no dusk – no proper time of day—
No sky – no earthly view—
No distance looking blue—
No road – no street – no 't' other side the way'—
No end to any Row—
No indications where the Crescents go—
No top to any steeple—
No recognitions of familiar people—
No courtesies for showing 'em—
No knowing 'em!—
No travelling at all – no locomotion,
No inkling of the way – no notion—
'No go' – by land or ocean—
No mail – no post—
No news from any foreign coast—
No Park – no Ring – no afternoon gentility—
No company – no nobility—
No warmth, no cheerfulness, no healthful ease,

No comfortable feel in any member—
No shade, no shine, no butterflies, no bees,
No fruits, no flowers, no leaves, no birds,—
November!

OGDEN NASH

(see page 96 for biography)

$\boxed{49}$

ENGLAND EXPECTS

Let us pause to consider the English,
Who when they pause to consider themselves they get
   all reticently thrilled and tinglish,
Because every Englishman is convinced of one thing,
   viz:
That to be an Englishman is to belong to the most
   exclusive club there is:
A club to which benighted bounders of Frenchmen and
   Germans and Italians et cetera cannot even aspire to
   belong,
Because they don't even speak English, and the Americans
   are worst of all because they speak it wrong.
Englishmen are distinguished by their traditions and
   ceremonials,
And also by their affection for their colonies and their
   contempt for the colonials.
When foreigners ponder world affairs, why sometimes
   by doubts they are smitten,
But Englishmen know instinctively that what the world
   needs most is whatever is best for Great Britain.

They have a splendid navy and they conscientiously
   admire it,
And every English schoolboy knows that John Paul Jones
   was only an unfair American pirate.
English people disclaim sparkle and verve,
But speak without reservations of their Anglo-Saxon
   reserve.
After listening to little groups of English ladies and
   gentlemen at cocktail parties and in hotels and
  Pullmans, of defining Anglo-Saxon reserve I despair,
But I think it consists of assuming that nobody else
   is there,
And I shudder to think where Anglo-Saxon reserve ends
   when I consider where it begins,
Which in a few high-pitched statements of what one's
   income is and just what foods give one a rash and
   whether one and one's husband or wife sleep in a
   double bed or twins.
All good Englishmen go to Oxford or Cambridge and they
   all write and publish books before their graduation,
And I often wondered how they did it until I realised
   that they have to do it because their genteel accents are
   so developed that they can no longer understand each
   other's spoken words so the written word is their only
   means of intercommunication.
England is the last home of the aristocracy, and the art
   of protecting the aristocracy from the encroachments of
   commerce has been raised to quite an art.
Because in America a rich butter-and-egg man is only a
   rich butter-and-egg man or at most an honorary LLD of

some hungry university, but in England he is Sir Benjamin
Buttery, Bart.
Anyhow, I think the English people are sweet,
And we might as well get used to them because when
they slip and fall they always land on their own or
somebody else's feet.

Blame the Vicar – John Betjeman

This light-hearted look at the local incumbent first appeared in *Poems in the Porch* in 1954 along with 'Diary of a Church Mouse' (see page 13 for details) and four other poems.

50

BLAME THE VICAR

When things go wrong it's rather tame
To find we are ourselves to blame,
It gets the trouble over quicker
To go and blame things on the Vicar.
The Vicar, after all, is paid
To keep us bright and undismayed.
The Vicar is more virtuous too
Than lay folks such as me and you.
He never swears, he never drinks,
He never *should* say what he thinks.
His collar is the wrong way round,
And that is why he's simply bound
To be the sort of person who
Has nothing very much to do
But take the blame for what goes wrong
And sing in tune at Evensong.
   For what's a Vicar really for
Except to cheer us up? What's more,
He shouldn't ever, ever tell
If there is such a place as Hell,
For if there is it's certain he
Will go to it as well as we.
The Vicar should be all pretence
And never, never give offence.
To preach on Sunday is his task

And lend his mower when we ask
And organise our village fêtes
And sing at Christmas with the waits
And in his car to give us lifts
And when we quarrel, heal the rifts.
To keep his family alive
He should industriously strive
In that enormous house he gets,
And he should always pay his debts,
For he has quite six pounds a week,
And when we're rude he should be meek
And always turn the other cheek.
He should be neat and nicely dressed
With polished shoes and trousers pressed,
For we look up to him as higher
Than anyone, except the Squire.

Dear People, who have read so far,
I know how really kind you are,
I hope that you are always seeing
Your Vicar as a human being,
Making allowances when he
Does things with which you don't agree.
But there are lots of people who
Are not so kind to him as you.
So in conclusion you shall hear
About a parish somewhat near,
Perhaps your own or maybe not,
And of the Vicars that it got.
One parson came and people said,

'Alas! Our former Vicar's dead!
And this new man is far more "Low"
Than dear old Reverend so-and-so,
And far too earnest in his preaching,
We do not really like his teaching,
He seems to think we're simply fools
Who've never been to Sunday Schools.'
That Vicar left, and by and by
A new one came, 'He's much too "High",'
The people said, 'too like a saint,
His incense makes our Mavis faint.'
So now he's left and they're alone
Without a Vicar of their own.
The living's been amalgamated
With one next door they've always hated.

STANLEY HOLLOWAY
1890–1982

───── ⚬⚬⚬ ─────

Born in London in 1890, he worked as an office boy and sang solo in a choir before becoming a lieutenant during the First World War.

He made his London stage debut in *Kissing Time* in 1919 at the Winter Garden, going on to star in *The Co-optimists* (the Royalty, 1921), *Fine and Dandy* (Saville, 1942), *Hit the Deck* (Hippodrome, 1927), *My Fair Lady* (Drury Lane, 1958), *Song of the Sea* (His Majesty's, 1928), *Three Sisters* (Drury Lane, 1934) and *Up and Doing* (Saville, 1940).

Holloway's films include *Passport to Pimlico* (1948), *The Lavender Hill Mob* (1951) and *My Fair Lady* (1964). His autobiography, *Wiv a Little Bit of Luck*, was published in 1969. Stanley Holloway died in 1982.

51

OLD SAM

It occurred on the evening before Waterloo
And troops were lined up on Parade,
And Sergeant inspecting 'em, he was a terror
Of whom every man was afraid—

All excepting one man who was in the front rank,
A man by the name of Sam Small,
And 'im and the Sergeant were both 'daggers drawn',
They thought 'nowt' of each other at all.

As Sergeant walked past he was swinging his arm,
And he happened to brush against Sam,
And knocking his musket clean out of his hand
It fell to the ground with a slam.

'Pick it oop,' said Sergeant, abrupt like but cool,
But Sam with a shake of his head
Said, 'Seeing as tha' knocked it out of me hand,
P'raps tha'll pick the thing oop instead.'

'Sam, Sam, pick oop tha' musket,'
The Sergeant exclaimed with a roar.
Sam said 'Tha' knocked it doon, Reet!
Then tha'll pick it oop, or it stays where it is, on't floor.'

The sound of high words
Very soon reached the ears of an Officer, Lieutenant Bird,
Who says to the Sergeant, 'Now what's all this 'ere?'
And the Sergeant told what had occurred.

'Sam, Sam, pick oop tha' musket,'
Lieutenant exclaimed with some heat.
Sam said 'He knocked it doon, Reet! then he'll pick it oop,
Or it stays where it is, at me feet.'

It caused quite a stir when the Captain arrived
To find out the cause of the trouble;
And every man there, all excepting Old Sam,
Was full of excitement and bubble.

'Sam, Sam, pick oop tha' musket,'
Said Captain for strictness renowned.
Sam said 'He knocked it doon, Reet!
Then he'll pick it oop, or it stays where it is on't ground.'

The same thing occurred when the Major and Colonel
Both tried to get Sam to see sense,
But when Old Duke o' Wellington came into view
Well, the excitement was tense.

Up rode the Duke on a lovely white 'orse,
To find out the cause of the bother;
He looks at the musket and then at Old Sam
And he talked to Old Sam like a brother,

'Sam, Sam, pick oop tha' musket,'
The Duke said as quiet as could be,
'Sam, Sam, pick oop tha' musket
Coom on, lad, just to please me.'

'Alright, Duke,' said Old Sam, 'just for thee I'll oblige,
And to show thee I meant no offence.'
So Sam picked it up, 'Gradeley, lad,' said the Duke,
'Right-o, boys, let battle commence.'

LEWIS CARROLL

(*see page 9 for biography*)

52

THE LOBSTER-QUADRILLE

'Will you walk a little faster?' said a whiting to a snail,
'There's a porpoise close behind us, and he's treading
    on my tail.
See how eagerly the lobsters and the turtles all advance!
They are waiting on the shingle – will you come and join
    the dance?
Will you, won't you, will you, won't you, will you join
    the dance?
Will you, won't you, will you, won't you, won't you join
    the dance?

'You can really have no notion how delightful it will be
When they take us up and throw us, with the lobsters,
    out to sea!'
But the snail replied 'Too far, too far!' and gave a look
    askance—
Said he thanked the whiting kindly, but he would not
    join the dance.
    Would not, could not, would not, could not, could not
        join the dance.
    Would not, could not, would not, could not, could not
        join the dance.

'What matters it how far we go?' his scaly friend replied.
'There is another shore, you know, upon the other side.
The further off from England, the nearer is to France.
Then turn not pale, beloved snail, but come and join
   the dance.
   Will you, won't you, will you, won't you, will you join
     the dance?
   Will you, won't you, will you, won't you, will you join
     the dance?'

SPIKE MILLIGAN
born 1918

———⬡⬡⬡———

Born in India, Spike Milligan is best known for his hilarious, innovative scripts for *The Goon Show*, first performed on the BBC in 1951. He played Eccles, and with Peter Sellers, Harry Secombe and Michael Bentine created a show which ran for nine years, revolutionised British comedy and achieved worldwide celebrity for all the participants.

Milligan has written many books of poetry and a multi-volume autobiography which includes the evocatively titled *Hitler: My Part in his Downfall*.

53

AGNUS DEI

Behold, behold,
The Lamb of God
As it skips and hops.
I know that soon
The Lamb of God
Will be the Lamb of Chops.

EDWARD LEAR

Edward Lear was the first person to put a collection of limericks together, in 1820, but they seem to have been invented in the eighteenth century. I recently discovered one that is very appropriate for Classic *f*M:

> *A tutor who taught on the flute*
> *Tried to teach two tooters to toot*
> *Said the two to the tutor*
> *'Is it harder to toot, or*
> *To tutor two tutors to toot?*

All sorts of people, including W. S. Gilbert, have tried their hand at them, and there are many anonymous – and often extremely rude – limericks to choose from, but the choice in our Top One Hundred is by the master himself, Edward Lear.

54

There was an old man who supposed
That the street door was partially closed;
But some very large rats
Ate his coat and his hats,
While that futile old gentleman dozed.

GEORGE STRONG
1832–1912

———◁∞∞▷———

George Strong is something of a mystery man. All we can find out is that he was American and obviously a witty man: *The Modern Hiawatha* is taken from a work called *The Song of Milkanwatha*.

55

THE MODERN HIAWATHA

When he killed the Mudjokivis,
Of the skin he made him mittens,
Made them with the fur side inside,
Made them with the skin side outside,
He, to get the warm side inside,
Put the inside skin side outside;
He, to get the cold side outside,
Put the warm side fur side inside.
That's why he put fur side inside,
Why he put the skin side outside,
Why he turned them inside outside.

W. M. PRAED

(see page 126 for biography)

[56]

THE TALENTED MAN

Dear Alice! you'll laugh when you know it,—
    Last week, at the Duchess's ball,
I danced with the clever new poet,—
    You've heard of him,— Tully St. Paul.
Miss Jonquil was perfectly frantic;
    I wish you had seen Lady Anne!
It really was very romantic,
    He *is* such a talented man!

He came up from Brazenose College,
    Just caught, as they call it, this spring;
And his head, love, is stuffed full of knowledge
    Of every conceivable thing.
Of science and logic he chatters,
    As fine and as fast as he can;
Though I am no judge of such matters,
    I'm sure he's a talented man.

His stories and jests are delightful;—
   Not stories or jests, dear, for you;
The jests are exceedingly spiteful,
   The stories not always *quite* true.
Perhaps to be kind and veracious
   May do pretty well at Lausanne;
But it never would answer,—good gracious!
   Chez nous—in a talented man.

He sneers,—how my Alice would scold him!—
   At the bliss of a sigh or a tear;
He laughed—only think!—when I told him
   How we cried o'er Trevelyan last year;
I vow I was quite in a passion;
   I broke all the sticks of my fan;
But sentiment's quite out of fashion,
   It seems, in a talented man.

Lady Bab, who is terribly moral,
   Has told me that Tully is vain,
And apt—which is silly—to quarrel,
   And fond—which is sad—of champagne,
I listened, and doubted, dear Alice,
   For I saw, when my Lady began,
It was only the Dowager's malice;—
   She *does* hate a talented man!

He's hideous, I own it. But fame, love,
  Is all that these eyes can adore;
He's lame,—but Lord Byron was lame, love,
  And dumpy,—but so is Tom Moore.
Then his voice,—*such* a voice! my sweet creature,
  It's like your Aunt Lucy's toucan:
But oh! what's a tone or a feature,
  When once one's a talented man?

My mother, you know, all the season,
  Has talked of Sir Geoffrey's estate;
And truly, to do the fool reason,
  He *has* been less horrid of late.
But today, when we drive in the carriage,
  I'll tell her to lay down her plan;—
If ever I venture on marriage,
  It must be a talented man!

P.S.—I have found, on reflection,
  One fault in my friend,—*entre nous*;
Without it, he'd just be perfection;—
  Poor fellow, he has not a *sou*!
And so, when he comes in September
  To shoot with my uncle, Sir Dan,
I've promised mamma to remember
  He's *only* a talented man!

My Busseductress – Roger McGough

Recorded as a song by Scaffold, the hit-making trio that comprised McGough, John Gorman and Mike McGear (McCartney). Bus conductresses (and bus fantasies) were a daily feature in the life of the young McGough, a serial bus passenger. Maybe he should have taken that driving test.

57

MY BUSSEDUCTRESS

She is as beautiful as bustickets
and smells of old cash
drinks Guinness off duty
eats sausage and mash.
But like everyone else
she has her busdreams too
when the peakhour is over
and there's nothing to do.

A fourposter upstairs
a juke-box inside
there are more ways than one
of enjoying a ride.
Velvet curtains on the windows
thick carpets on the floor
roulette under the stairs
a bar by the door.

Three times a day
she'd perform a strip-tease
and during the applause
say nicely 'fares please'.
Upstairs she'd reserve
for men of her choice
invite them along
in her best clippie voice.

She knows it sounds silly
what would the police say
but thinks we'd be happier
if she had her way.
There are so many youngmen
she'd like to know better
give herself with the change
if only they'd let her.

She is as beautiful as bustickets
and smells of old cash
drinks Guinness off duty
eats sausage and mash.
But she has her busdreams
hot and nervous
my blueserged queen
of the transport service.

WENDY COPE
born 1945

————⊛————

Born in 1945, Wendy Mary Cope attended Farrington's School, Chislehurst, and St Hilda's, Oxford, before training as a teacher at Westminster College, Oxford. She worked as a teacher prior to becoming the television columnist for the *Spectator*, a position which she held from 1986 to 1990. Her first poetry book was *Making Cocoa for Kingsley Amis* (1986), followed by a book of children's poems, *Twiddling Your Thumbs* (1988), *The River Girl* (1991) and *Serious Concerns* (1992).

58

LONELY HEARTS

Can someone make my simple wish come true?
Male biker seeks female for touring fun.
Do you live in North London? Is it you?

Gay vegetarian whose friends are few,
I'm into music, Shakespeare and the sun.
Can someone make my simple wish come true?

Executive in search of something new—
Perhaps bisexual woman, arty, young.
Do you live in North London? Is it you?

Successful, straight and solvent? I am too—
Attractive Jewish lady with a son.
Can someone make my simple wish come true?

I'm Libran, inexperienced and blue—
Need slim non-smoker, under twenty-one.
Do you live in North London? Is it you?

Please write (with photo) to Box 152
Who knows where it may lead once we've begun?
Can someone make my simple wish come true?
Do you live in North London? Is it you?

OGDEN NASH

(see page 96 for biography)

|59|

CURL UP AND DIET

Some ladies smoke too much and some ladies drink too
  much and some ladies pray too much,
But all ladies think that they weigh too much.
They may be as slender as a sylph or a dryad,
But just let them get on the scales and they embark on
  a doleful jeremiad:
No matter how low the figure the needle happens to
  touch,
They always claim it is at least five pounds too much;
To the world she may appear slinky and feline,
But she inspects herself in the mirror and cries, Oh, I look
  like a sea lion.
Yes, she tells you she is growing into the shape of a sea
  cow or manatee,
And if you say No, my dear, she says you are just lying
  to make her feel better, and if you say Yes, my dear,
    you injure her vanity.
Once upon a time there was a girl more beautiful and
  witty and charming than tongue can tell,

And she is now a dangerous raving maniac in a
    padded cell,
And the first indication her friends and relatives had that
    she was mentally overwrought
Was one day when she said, I weigh a hundred and
    twenty-seven, which is exactly what I ought.
Oh, often I am haunted
By the thought that somebody might someday discover
    a diet that would let ladies reduce just as much as they
    wanted,
Because I wonder if there is a woman in the world
    strong-minded enough to shed ten pounds or twenty,
And say There now, that's plenty;
And I fear me one ten-pound loss would only arouse the
    craving for another,
So it wouldn't do any good for ladies to get their ambition
    and look like somebody's fourteen-year-old brother,
Because, having accomplished this with ease,
They would next want to look like somebody's fourteen-
year-old brother in the final stages of some obscure
    disease,
And the more success you have the more you want to
    get of it,
So then their goal would be to look like somebody's
    fourteen-year-old brother's ghost, or rather not the ghost
    itself, which is fairly solid, but a silhouette of it,
So I think it is very nice for ladies to be lithe and
    lissome.
But not so much so that you cut yourself if you happen
    to embrace or kissome.

PHILIP LARKIN
1922–85

———— ∞∞∞ ————

Philip Larkin was born in Coventry on 9 August 1922, the son of the City Treasurer. He attended the King Henry VIII School before going up to St John's College, Oxford, where he met Kingsley Amis, the future novelist and poet, who became his close friend. After university he became a librarian, first at Leicester University, then in Belfast, and finally in Hull, where he moved in 1955 and where he was to remain until the end of his life. He published his first volume of poetry in 1945 and ten years later had become a poet of some standing, often being bracketed with Kingsley Amis and John Wain as writers whose love of poetry was mingled with a love of jazz.

Larkin never married, but shared his life in Hull from 1974 with Monica Jones. As he grew older, frustrated by increasing deafness, he wrote little poetry. On the death of his friend John Betjeman in 1984 he was invited to become Poet Laureate but, despite his admiration for the Prime Minister, Margaret Thatcher, he declined. Within a year Larkin followed Betjeman to the grave. Although his Will specifically stated that all his papers should be burned, his instructions were contradictory and so were not carried out.

60

ANNUS MIRABILIS

Sexual intercourse began
In nineteen sixty-three
(Which was rather late for me)—
Between the end of the *Chatterley* ban
And the Beatles' first LP.

Up till then there'd only been
A sort of bargaining,
A wrangle for a ring,
A shame that started at sixteen
And spread to everything.

Then all at once the quarrel sank:
Everyone felt the same,
And every life became
A brilliant breaking of the bank,
A quite unlosable game.

So life was never better than
In nineteen sixty-three
(Though just too late for me)—
Between the end of the *Chatterley* ban
And the Beatles' first LP.

G. K. CHESTERTON

(see page 39 for biography)

(see page 39 for biography)

61

THE SONG AGAINST GROCERS

God made the wicked Grocer
For a mystery and a sign,
That men might shun the awful shops
And go to inns to dine;
Where the bacon's on the rafter
And the wine is in the wood,
And God that made good laughter
Has seen that they are good.

The evil-hearted Grocer
Would call his mother 'Ma'am,'
And bow at her and bob at her,
Her aged soul to damn,
And rub his horrid hands and ask
What article was next,
Though *mortis in articulo*
Should be her proper text.

His props are not his children,
But pert lads underpaid,
Who call out 'Cash!' and bang about
To work his wicked trade;
He keeps a lady in a cage
Most cruelly all day,
And makes her count and calls her
'Miss'
Until she fades away.

The righteous minds of innkeepers
Induce them now and then
To crack a bottle with a friend
Or treat unmoneyed men,
But who hath seen the Grocer
Treat housemaids to his teas
Or crack a bottle of fish sauce
Or stand a man a cheese?

He sells us sands of Araby
As sugar for cash down;
He sweeps his shop and sells the dust
The purest salt in town,
He crams with cans of poisoned meat
Poor subjects of the King,
And when they die by thousands
Why, he laughs like anything.

The wicked Grocer groces
In spirits and in wine,
Not frankly and in fellowship
As men in inns do dine;
But packed with soap and sardines
And carried off by grooms,
For to be snatched by Duchesses
And drunk in dressing-rooms.

The hell-instructed Grocer
Has a temple made of tin,
And the ruin of good innkeepers
Is loudly urged therein;
But now the sands are running out
From sugar of a sort,
The Grocer trembles; for his time,
Just like his weight, is short.

CLIVE JAMES
born 1939

———— ∞ ————

Clive Vivien Leopold James was born in Sydney, Australia, in 1939, where he attended Sydney Technical High School and majored in psychology at the University.

In 1963 he moved to London, and took a variety of jobs before going to Pembroke College, Cambridge, where he became president of the Cambridge Footlights. In 1972 he was taken on by the *Observer* as their television critic, a post he held for ten years, whist building his career as a writer and graduating as a television presenter and interviewer.

As well as being a prolific writer of successful novels, literary criticism and poetry, he also made forays into lyric writing, providing the words for songs by singer/song-writer Pete Atkin.

The Book of My Enemy Has Been Remaindered
– Clive James

Clive James's early verse was published under the pseudonym of Edward Pygge, but this four-verse poem was written in 1983 and included in his 1986 collection *Other Passports. Poems 1958–1985*.

62

THE BOOK OF MY ENEMY HAS BEEN REMAINDERED

The book of my enemy has been remaindered
And I am pleased.
In vast quantities it has been remaindered.
Like a van-load of counterfeit that has been seized
And sits in piles in a police warehouse,
My enemy's much-prized effort sits in piles
In the kind of bookshop where remaindering occurs.
Great, square stacks of rejected books and, between
    them, aisles
One passes down reflecting on life's vanities,
Pausing to remember all those thoughtful reviews
Lavished to no avail upon one's enemy's book—
For behold, here is that book
Among these ranks and banks of duds,
These ponderous and seemingly irreducible cairns
Of complete stiffs.

The book of my enemy has been remaindered
And I rejoice.
It has gone with bowed head like a defeated legion
Beneath the yoke.
What avail him now his awards and prizes,
The praise expended upon his meticulous technique,
His individual new voice?
Knocked into the middle of next week

James

His brainchild now consorts with the bad buys,
The sinkers, clinkers, dogs and dregs,
The Edsels of the world of movable type,
The bummers that no amount of hype could shift,
The unbudgeable turkeys.

Yea, his slim volume with its understated wrapper
Bathes in the glare of the brightly jacketed *Hitler's War
    Machine*
His unmistakably individual new voice
Shares the same scrapyard with a forlorn skyscraper
Of *The Kung-Fu Cookbook*,
His honesty, proclaimed by himself and believed in
    by others,
His renowned abhorrence of all posturing and pretence,
Is there with *Pertwee's Promenades and Pierrots—
One Hundred Years of Seaside Entertainment*,
And (oh, this above all) his sensibility,
His sensibility and its hair-like filaments,
His delicate, quivering sensibility is now as one
With *Barbara Windsor's Book of Boobs*,
A volume graced by the descriptive rubric
'My boobs will give everyone hours of fun.'

Soon now a book of mine could be remaindered also,
Though not to the monumental extent
In which the chastisement of remaindering has been
    meted out
To the book of my enemy,
Since in the case of my own book it will be due

To a miscalculated print run, a marketing error—
Nothing to do with merit.
But just supposing that such an event should hold
Some slight element of sadness, it will be offset
By the memory of this sweet moment.
Chill the champagne and polish the crystal goblets!
The book of my enemy has been remaindered
And I am glad.

KENNETH GRAHAME

(*see page* 77 *for biography*)

63

DUCKS' DITTY

All along the backwater,
Through the rushes tall,
Ducks are a-dabbling,
Up tails all!

Ducks' tails, drakes' tails,
Yellow feet a-quiver,
Yellow bills all out of sight
Busy in the river!

Slushy green undergrowth
Where the roach swim—
Here we keep our larder,
Cool and full and dim.

Every one for what he likes!
We like to be
Heads down, tails up,
Dabbling free!

High in the blue above
Swifts whirl and call—
We are down a-dabbling
Up tails all!

HUGO WILLIAMS
born 1942

———— ∞∞∞ ————

The son of actor Hugh Williams, he was born in Windsor in 1942 and educated at Eton. He worked on the *London Magazine* as editorial assistant before travelling around the world. His first book of poems, *Symptoms of Loss*, was published in 1965, followed by his book *All the Time in the World* (1966). He had a second spell on the *London Magazine*, where he stayed until 1970. That same year his second book of poems, *Sugar Daddy*, was published. His other poetry books include *Some Sweet Day* (1975), *Love Life* (1979) and *Writing Home* (1985). In 1989 Williams himself chose poems from his five books for *Selected Poems*. Edna Longley in the *Irish Times* referred to him as 'possibly the most original poet of his generation in England'. In 1990 *Self Portrait with a Slide* was published.

New Ground – Hugo Williams

This poem comes from Hugo Williams's 1985 collection *Writing Home*, which was a Poetry Society Choice that year. The book is dedicated to his mother; the poem is about his father.

64

NEW GROUND

We played Scrabble wrong for years.
We counted the Double and Triple Word Scores
as often as we liked.
We had to move aside the letters
to see what colours they were on.

My father was out of work
and we were moving again. He stared at the board,
twisting his signet ring.
He liked adding 's' to a word
and scoring more points
than the person who thought of it.

He wanted 'chinas'. He said they were ornamental
bricks from Derbyshire, hand-painted.
He cheated from principle, to open up new ground
for his family. Not 'God feeds the ravens',
but *Mundum mea patria est*. We were stuck

at the end of a lane in Sussex
for two winters. My father threw down
his high-scoring spelling mistakes and bluffs
and started counting.
He would have walked all over us
if we'd let him have the last word—

'aw' as in 'Aw, hell!', 'ex' with the 'x' falling
on the last Triple Letter Score.
We made him take everything back.
What was left in his hand counted against him.

ADRIAN HENRI
born 1932

———◈———

Born in Birkenhead in 1932, Adrian Maurice Henri moved at the age of six, with his family, to Rhyl in North Wales. He attended the St Asaph Grammar School before going on to King's College, Durham, in 1951 to study Fine Art. After leaving in 1955, he was employed as a teacher, spending summers working on the fairground at Rhyl.

In the late 1950s he worked as a scenic artist at Liverpool Playhouse while he blossomed as a painter. From 1961 to 1968 he lectured at Manchester and Liverpool art colleges. He performed and wrote poetry, which led to him, Roger McGough and Brian Patten being dubbed 'the Liverpool poets'. From 1968 to 1970 Henri led a poetry/rock group – 'The Liverpool Scene'. Since then he has freelanced as writer, painter, performer, teacher, children's author and dramatist.

65

LOVE IS . . .

Love is feeling cold in the back of vans
Love is a fanclub with only two fans
Love is walking holding paintstained hands
Love is

Love is fish and chips on winter nights
Love is blankets full of strange delights
Love is when you don't put out the light
Love is

Love is the presents in Christmas shops
Love is when you're feeling Top of the Pops
Love is what happens when the music stops
Love is

Love is white panties lying all forlorn
Love is a pink nightdress still slightly warm
Love is when you have to leave at dawn
Love is

Love is you and love is me
Love is a prison and love is free
Love's what's there when you're away from me
Love is . . .

WILLIAM COWPER
1731–1800

Cowper was born in the parsonage of Great Berkhampsted, Hertfordshire, in 1731, the elder son of the rector. His mother died when he was six years old, and he attended a private school at Market Street, Hertfordshire, before going on to Westminster School.

On leaving, he was articled to a solicitor by the name of Chapman for three years, before entering the Inner Temple as a regular law student. He was called to the Bar but melancholia led him to being committed to the care of Dr Cotton of St Albans, his state of mind not being helped by having his hopes of marrying his cousin, Theodora, dashed.

In 1765 he lived in the Huntingdon house of the Reverend Morley Unwin as his adopted son, marrying his wife after the incumbent's death. Cowper wrote prolifically, but following his wife's death in 1796 he fell into a deep depression; guilt and paranoia continuing to affect his mental state. In his memoir he wrote 'conviction of sin and expectation of instant judgement never left me'.

Cowper died in 1800. He is probably one of the least likely poets to feature in a top hundred list of humorous poems!

66

TO THE IMMORTAL MEMORY OF THE HALIBUT
ON WHICH I DINED THIS DAY, MONDAY,
APRIL 26, 1784

Where hast thou floated, in what seas pursued
Thy pastime? when wast thou an egg new spawn'd,
Lost in th'immensity of ocean's waste?
Roar as they might, the overbearing winds
That rock'd the deep, thy cradle, thou wast safe—
And in thy minikin and embryo state,
Attach'd to the firm leaf of some salt weed,
Didst outlive tempests, such as wrung and rack'd
The joints of many a stout and gallant bark,
And whelm'd them in the unexplored abyss.
Indebted to no magnet and no chart,
Nor under guidance of the polar fire,
Thou wast a voyager on many coasts,
Grazing at large in meadows submarine,
Where flat Batavia, just emerging, peeps
Above the brine – where Caledonia's rocks
Beat back the surge – and where Hibernia shoots
Her wondrous causeway far into the main.
—Wherever thou hast fed, thou little thought'st,
And I not more, that I should feed on thee.
Peace, therefore, and good health, and much good fish
To him who sent thee! and success, as oft
As it descends into the billowy gulf,

To the same drag that caught thee! – Fare thee well!
Thy lot thy brethren of the slimy fin
Would envy, could they know that thou wast doom'd
To feed a bard, and to be praised in verse.

NIGEL FORDE

(*see page 167 for biography*)

67

VILLAGE CRICKET
OR
THE NON-PLAYER TROPHY

The village green and two o'the clock;
A perfect day for sport,
Where, like a country proverb,
The scoreboard says 'nought for nought';
And A. G. MacDonell's shade shakes hands
With Hugh de Selincourt.

The hedges are choked with briar rose
Above the listless pools
Where dragonflies flash like veins of sun
And gnats model molecules,
And the umpire sucks his pipe and studies
The LBW rules.

This is just swank: he suffers from
Myopia, arthritis and gout,
And he's long since given up trying to be fair
Or tempering bias with doubt;
He works by the law of averages—
Every fifth appeal is 'out'.

The side consists of a postman, a printer,
An out-of-work jazz musician;
Two farmers, two teachers, a sales rep, a clerk
And an overweight obstetrician
Who's forged a Surrey sweater just
To frighten the opposition.

The pitch is thick with daisies and dock,
Toadstooled and pitted with holes;
It's laid on last season's football pitch—
Just in front of one of the goals.
The batsman's only real defence
Is by courtesy of the moles.

'Deep extra cover, Jim; Ray, at point',
Says the captain, a bit tongue in cheek;
He looked up the technical terms last night
And remembered them, too, by some freak;
But nobody knows what he's talking about
So they go where they went last week.

The village aged sit around
And draw lots for whose turn to recall
The day young Hubert clouted a six
Right over the churchyard wall;
And express their regret that this pansy set
Has no sense of tradition at all.

There's the one with the dreadful fear of the ball
Who stands on the boundary
And makes quite sure that the sun's in his eyes
And a catch will be hard to see;
He's worked out how to miss it by half an inch
And fall spectacularly.

The wicketkeeper smacks his gloves
In anticipatory glee;
Like Alan Knott, he moves a lot,
Waves arms and bends the knee;
And like the Ancient Mariner,
He stoppeth one of three.

The obstetrician's Lancia stands,
Its bodywork ticks in the sun;
It's the bodywork of its passenger that
Inspires the outfield to run.
She sits bored, sunglasses in her hair,
And listens to Radio 1.

Small children pester the batting side
As small horseflies pester stallions;
Linseed oil and new-mown grass
Bloom on the air. Batallions
Of Ian Botham look-unlikes
Strut round behind medallions.

Wives and girlfriends gossip and giggle
And clatter and clink and clup
As they chop and spread and slice and cut
And the sandwiches greyly pile up;
And they brew that deadly orange tea
That sets when it hits the cup.

It's during tea that the dog appears
From the depths of a shady thicket;
He pads across and sniffs the stumps
Then cocks his leg at the wicket,
No player and no gentleman,
But a connoisseur of cricket.

P. G. WODEHOUSE
1881–1975

Born Pelham Grenville Wodehouse in Guildford, Surrey, in 1881, as a baby he lived in Hong Kong, where his father was a judge. When Pelham was two, he and his brothers were sent back to England, where he lived with a succession of aunts. On leaving Dulwich College, he worked in a London bank for two years, before leaving in 1903 to work for the London *Globe*. He had already achieved some success as a freelance writer, his first novel being published in 1902. His most famous creations were Bertie Wooster and his manservant Jeeves, who first appeared in a collection of short stories in 1919. Wodehouse first visited the United States in 1904, where he had considerable success as a lyricist with the Gershwins, Jerome Kern and Guy Bolton, writing for such shows as *Sitting Pretty* and *O, Kay!* and *Show Boat*.

From 1934 Wodehouse and wife Ethel lived in the South of France. During the Second World War, the Germans persuaded him to broadcast on German radio. Despite their innocuous nature, the broadcasts created such a reaction in Britain that he settled in the USA. He was knighted weeks before his death in 1975 aged ninety-three.

68

PRINTER'S ERROR

As o'er my latest book I pored,
   Enjoying it immensely,
I suddenly exclaimed 'Good Lord!'
   And gripped the volume tensely.
'Golly!' I cried. I writhed in pain.
'They've done it on me once again!'
   And furrows creased my brow.
I'd written (which I thought quite good)
'Ruth, ripening into womanhood,
Was now a girl who knocked men flat
And frequently got whistled at',
And some vile, careless, casual gook
Had spoiled the best thing in the book
   By printing 'not'
   (Yes, 'not', great Scott!)
   When I had written 'now'.

On murder in the first degree
   The Law, I knew, is rigid:
Its attitude, if A kills B,
   To A is always frigid.
It counts it not a trivial slip
If on behalf of authorship
You liquidate compositors.
This kind of conduct it abhors

235

And seldom will allow.
Nevertheless, I deemed it best
And in the public interest
To buy a gun, to oil it well,
Inserting what is called a shell,
     And go and pot
     With sudden shot
     This printer who had printed 'not'
     When I had written 'now'.

I tracked the bounder to his den
     Through private information:
I said, 'Good afternoon', and then
     Explained the situation:
'I'm not a fussy man,' I said.
'I smile when you put "rid" for "red"
And "bad" for "bed" and "hoad" for "head"
     And "bolge" instead of "bough".
When "wone" appears in lieu of "wine"
Or if you alter "Cohn" to "Schine",
     I never make a row.
I know how easy errors are.
But this time you have gone too far
By printing "not" when you knew what
     I really wrote was "now".
Prepare,' I said, 'to meet your God
Or, as you'd say, your Goo or Bod,
     Or possibly your Gow.'

A few weeks later into court
  I came to stand my trial.
The Judge was quite a decent sort.
  He said, 'Well, cocky, I'll
Be passing sentence in a jiff,
And so, my poor unhappy stiff,
If you have anything to say,
Now is the moment. Fire away.
  You have?'
  I said, 'And how!
Me lud, the facts I don't dispute.
I did, I own it freely, shoot
This printer through the collar stud.
What else could I have done, me lud?
  He'd printed "not" . . .'
  The judge said, '*What!*
  When you had written "now"?
God bless my soul! Gadzooks!' said he.
'The blighters did that once to me.
  A dirty trick, I trow.
I hereby quash and override
The jury's verdict. Gosh!' he cried.
'Give me your hand. Yes, I insist,
You splendid fellow! Case dismissed.'
  (Cheers, and a Voice 'Wow-wow!')

A statue stands against the sky,
   Lifelike and rather pretty.
'Twas recently erected by
   The PEN committee.
And many a passer-by is stirred,
For on the plinth, if that's the word,
In golden letters you may read
'This is the man who did the deed.
   His hand set to the plough,
He did not sheathe the sword, but got
A gun at great expense and shot
The human blot who'd printed "not"
   When he had written "now".
He acted with no thought of self,
Not for advancement, not for pelf,
But just because it made him hot
To think the man had printed "not"
   When he had written "now".'

Pot Pourri from a Surrey Garden – John Betjeman

During 1931 and early 1932 Betjeman had a strong crush on Pamela one of the Mitford girls. They socialised, went for drives and visited churches, and she admitted that she loved his company, was fond of him and he made her laugh, but she wasn't *in* love with him. He included her in a piece of nonsense verse about 'The Mitford Girls', the first time the phrase was used in print.

> *The Mitford Girls, the Mitford Girls*
> *I love them for their sins*
> *The younger ones like 'cavalcade'*
> *The old like maskelyns**
>
> *Sophistication, blessed dame*
> *Sure they have heard thy call*
> *Yes, even when gentle Pamela*
> *Most rural of them all!*

While he undoubtedly used the name and image of Pamela Mitford in 'Pot Pourri from a Surrey Garden', it is a fantasy piece in which he set somebody like her, as her brother Tom was at Eton not Malvern, and there is no church featuring the described architecture in Windlesham.

---

* *Cavalcade* was a Noël Coward comedy and Maskelyn a conjuror.

69

POT POURRI FROM A SURREY GARDEN

Miles of pram in the wind and Pam in the gorse track,
   Coco-nut smell of the broom and a packet of Weights
Press'd in the sand. The thud of a hoof on a horse-
   track—
A horse-riding horse for a horse-track—
     Conifer county of Surrey approached
Through remarkable wrought-iron gates.

Over your boundary now, I wash my face in a bird-bath,
   Then which path shall I take? That over there by
     the pram?
Down by the pond? or else, shall I take the slippery
   third path.
     Trodden away with gymn. shoes,
     Beautiful fir-dry alley that leads
To the bountiful body of Pam?

Pam, I adore you, Pam, you great big mountainous
   sports girl,
   Whizzing them over the net, full of the strength of
     five;
That old Malvernian brother, you zephyr and khaki
   shorts girl,
     Although he's playing for Woking,
Can't stand up to your wonderful backhand drive.

See the strength of her arm, as firm and hairy as
    Hendren's;
    See the size of her thighs, the pout of her lips as,
      cross,
And full of a pent-up strength, she swipes at the
    rhododendrons,
      Lucky the rhododendrons,
      And flings her arrogant love-lock
Back with a petulant toss.

Over the redolent pinewoods, in at the bathroom
    casement,
    One fine Saturday, Windlesham bells shall call
Up the Butterfield aisle rich with Gothic enlacement,
      Licensed now for embracement,
Pam and I, as the organ
    Thunders over you all.

E. J. THRIBB
C. 1970–

———— ✿ ————

The eternally youthful Thribb (17½) was the invention, *circa* 1970, of *Private Eye*'s Richard Ingrams and Barry Fantoni. A reclusive figure, with a friend called Keith, his initial poems were on a wider variety of topics than the 'In Memoriams' with which he found lasting fame. The relatives of the deceased celebrated in the short, stylised poems have invariably been touched by the Thribb tributes (i.e, Frank Muir's son and Donald Peer's widow). Written by a committee (no one person could safely shoulder the responsibility of wearing the Thribb mantle full time) the works of the enigmatic teenager have only been published once in book form, when *So farewell then* . . . hit the shops. As can be seen from his position at number 70 in the chart, where he nestles comfortably between John Betjeman and Barry Humphries – Thribb lives.

$\boxed{70}$

IN MEMORIAM
DIZZY GILLESPIE AND RUDOLPH NUREYEV

So. Farewell
Then

Dizzy Gillespie
Famous jazz
Trumpeter.

You were known
For your
Bulging cheeks

Rudolph Nureyev

So were
You.

BARRY HUMPHRIES
born 1934

—∞∞∞—

Born in Australia in 1934, Humphries, alias Dame Edna Everage, alias Les Patterson, is the son of a Victoria builder whose father emigrated to Australia in the 1880s.

Humphries attended Melbourne Grammar School and Melbourne University, before becoming an actor, and moved to Britain in 1959. He went on to star as Fagin in the West End musical *Oliver!*, as well as drawing a strip cartoon for *Private Eye* magazine, 'Barry McKenzie'.

He is best known for his female creation Dame Edna. Humphries was a great chum of fellow *One Hundred Favourite Humorous Poems* poet John Betjeman.

71

A MEGASTAR'S MANTRAS
THINGS THAT MEAN A LOT TO ME

A is for Australia,
The land I adore;
It's so spotless and clean
You can eat off the floor.

B is for Boomerang,
Which our quaint Abos launch
In the hope it will bring back
A roast quokka's haunch.

C is for Culture
Which blossoms unchecked,
You can't move in my homeland
For Beckett and Brecht.

D is for Dingo,
Our indigenous pup,
You just have to look at him
And he'll gobble you up.

E is for Explorer,
A brave little chap
Who helped put my wonderful land
On the map.

F is for Funnell-web
Our furry-legged foe.
He sleeps in your slipper
And breakfasts on toe.

G is for Gladdy, Ginseng, Galle glass,
It's also for Glyndebourne where you eat off the grass.
G stands for Gucci, James Galway, Gay Lib,
Gallipoli, Galliano, and the four brothers Gibb.
The Golden Goanna is our top film award
And with Genet and Günter Grass I'm never bored.
Glenda Jackson and Greta Garbo are Gs without peer,
So are Gough, Gary Glitter and our own Germaine Greer.
To hear Grace Jones sing I'd pay quite a lot for,
And Gaddafi's a socialist I've got a soft spot for.
G stands for Graffiti, a word that I veto
Since Mature Students have taught me to call it Graffito.
By the end of this poem I'm sure you'll agree
That I have a very soft G-spot for G!

H is for Harrods,
My favourite boutique;
If you shop there they'll treat you
Like a little-known sheik.

I is for invalid
Who'll never come home;
I've just given Norm's drip
A new coat of Chrome.

J is for Joylene,
My daughter-in-law;
In a jumpsuit she skates
On a black rubber floor.

K is for Kelly
Our radical Ned;
When none other dared
He wore a tin on his head.

L is for Leather
In sling-backs and mules,
You should see the accessories
My son's flatmate tools.

M is for Mould-breaking,
What I do best,
With the mould on Madge Allsop
I'm put to the test.

N is for Nivea
Where my digit oft dives;
Try it in a sandwich
With finely chopped chives.

O is for Opera House,
An Australian invention
Ideal for casino
Or business convention.

P is for Pizzazz
Which makes paupers happy,
They adore my charisma
And I'm raunchy and zappy!

Q is for Queen
Whom I know very well;
She's confided some scorchers
Which I doubt if I'll tell.

R is for Refinement
Which Australians exude,
Don't let some of our statesmen
Persuade you we're crude.

S is for Subsidies
The Arts Council keeps giving,
Thus sparing our authors
From writing books for a living.

T is for Thrush,
The name of a bird;
It's also a yukky old fungus
I've heard.

U is Urine
Say 'yuk' if you might;
Little jobs keep
Mother's hands soft and white.

V is for Valmai
My sensitive daughter;
She was uptight in Safeways
When security caught her.

W is for Woodwork
At which Madge is improving,
She keeps me awake
With her tonguing and grooving

X is for X-ellence,
Though it's not spelt that way;
It's my bottom line
At the end of the day.

Y is for The Yell,
And I've got a queer hunch
It's the most gorgeous thing
Ever painted by Munch.

Z is for Zero,
A mark I bestow
On once-famous women
Like Margaret Trudeau.

HILAIRE BELLOC

(see page 17 for biography)

[72]

LINES TO A DON

Remote and ineffectual Don
That dared attack my Chesterton,
With that poor weapon, half-impelled,
Unlearnt, unsteady, hardly held,
Unworthy for a tilt with men—
Your quavering and corroded pen;
Don poor at Bed and worse at Table,
Don pinched, Don starved, Don miserable;
Don stuttering, Don with roving eyes,
Don nervous, Don of crudities;
Don clerical, Don ordinary,
Don self-absorbed and solitary;
Don here-and-there, Don epileptic;
Don puffed-and empty, Don dyspeptic;
Don middle-class, Don sycophantic,
Don dull, Don brutish, Don pedantic;
Don hypocritical, Don bad,
Don furtive, Don three-quarters mad;
Don (since a man must make an end),
Don that shall never be my friend.

Don different from those regal Dons!
With hearts of gold and lungs of bronze,
Who shout and bang and roar and bawl
The Absolute across the hall,
Or sail in amply bellying gown
Enormous through the Sacred Town,
Bearing from College to their homes
Deep cargoes of gigantic tomes;
Dons admirable! Dons of Might!
Uprising on my inward sight
Compact of ancient tales, and port,
And sleep – and learning of a sort.
Dons English, worthy of the land;
Dons rooted; Dons that understand.
Good Dons perpetual that remain
A landmark, walling in the plain—
The horizon of my memories—
Like large and comfortable trees.

Don very much apart from these,
Thou scapegoat Don, thou Don devoted,
Don to thine own damnation quoted,
Perplexed to find thy trivial name
Reared in my verse to lasting shame.
Don dreadful, rasping Don and wearing,
Repulsive Don – Don past all bearing.
Don of the cold and doubtful breath,
Don despicable, Don of death;
Don nasty, skimpy, silent, level;
Don evil; Don that serves the devil.

Don ugly – that makes fifty lines.
There is a Canon which confines
A Rhymed Octosyllabic Curse
If written in Iambic Verse
To fifty lines. I never cut;
I far prefer to end it – but
Believe me I shall soon return.
My fires are banked, but still they burn
To write some more about the Don
That dared attack my Chesterton.

NOEL PETTY

—◦◦◦◦—

Noel Petty is a retired mathematician and an inveterate enterer of literary competitions, composer of parodies, squibs and other light verse. As Petty himself points out, 'all else is not really relevant'.

73

WHAT FOR!

One more word, said my dad,
And I'll give you what for.
What for? I said.
That's right, he said, what for!
No, I said, I mean what for?
What will you give me what for for?
Never you mind, he said. Wait and see.
But what is what for for? I said.
What's what for for? he said,
It's to teach you what's what,
That's what.
What's that? I said.
Right, he said, you're for it,
I'm going to let you have it.
Have what? I said.
Have what? he said,
What for, that's what.
Do you want me to really give you
Something to think about?
I don't know, I said,
I'm thinking about it.
Then he clipped me over the ear.
It was the first time he'd made sense
All day.

COLE PORTER
1891–1964

———— ∞∞∞ ————

Born in 1891 in Peru, Indiana, to a wealthy family, he studied piano and violin from an early age, later studying music at Harvard. During the First World War, he served in the French Army as an American citizen; he married in 1919 and lived in France for the next decade. He began to have success as a songwriter from the late 1920s.

Certainly one of the great songwriters of the century, his songs included 'Let's Do It', 'Don't Fence Me In', 'Anything Goes', 'I Get A Kick Out Of You', 'You're The Top', 'Every Time We Say Goodbye', 'In The Still Of The Night' and 'Well, Did You Evah?' Both Porter's legs were badly smashed in 1937 when a horse fell on him, resulting in countless operations to save his limbs. A semi-invalid for the rest of his life, his right leg was amputated in 1958.

Brush Up Your Shakespeare – Cole Porter

'Brush Up Your Shakespeare' comes from the musical *Kiss Me Kate* based on Shakespeare's *The Taming of the Shrew*, with music and lyrics by Cole Porter, which opened at the Coliseum in London on 8 March 1951.

74

BRUSH UP YOUR SHAKESPEARE

The girls today in society
Go for classical poetry
So to win their hearts one must quote with ease
Aeschylus and Euripides.
One must know Homer and, b'lieve me, bo,
Sophocles, also Sappho-ho.
Unless you know Shelley and Keats and Pope,
Dainty debbies will call you a dope.
But the poet of them all
Who will start 'em simply ravin'
Is the poet people call
'The bard of Stratford-on-Avon'.

Brush up your Shakespeare,
Start quoting him now,
Brush up your Shakespeare
And the women you will wow.
Just declaim a few lines from 'Othella'
And they'll think you're a helluva fella,
If your blonde won't respond when you flatter 'er
Tell her what Tony told Cleopaterer,
If she fights when her clothes you are mussing,
What are clothes? 'Much Ado About Nussing.'
Brush up your Shakespeare
And they'll all kowtow.

Brush up your Shakespeare,
Start quoting him now,
Brush up your Shakespeare
And the women you will wow.
With the wife of the British embessida
Try a crack out of 'Troilus and Cressida',
If she says she won't buy it or tike it
Make her tike it, what's more, 'As You Like It'.
If she says your behavior is heinous
Kick her right in the 'Coriolanus',
Brush up your Shakespeare
And they'll all kowtow.

Brush up your Shakespeare,
Start quoting him now,
Brush up your Shakespeare
And the women you will wow.
If you can't be a ham and do 'Hamlet'
They will not give a damn or a damnlet,
Just recite an occasional sonnet
And your lap'll have 'Honey' upon it,
When your baby is pleading for pleasure
Let her sample your 'Measure for Measure',
Brush up your Shakespeare
And they'll all kowtow.

Brush up your Shakespeare,
Start quoting him now,
Brush up your Shakespeare
And the women you will wow.

Better mention 'The Merchant of Venice'
When her sweet pound o' flesh you would menace,
If her virtue, at first, she defends – well,
Just remind her that 'All's Well That Ends Well',
And if still she won't give you a bonus
You know what Venus got from Adonis!
Brush up your Shakespeare
And they'll all kowtow.

Brush up your Shakespeare
Start quoting him now,
Brush up your Shakespeare
And the women you will wow.
If your goil is a Washington Heights dream
Treat the kid to 'A Midsummer Night's Dream',
If she then wants an all-by-herself night
Let her rest ev'ry 'leventh or 'Twelfth Night',
If because of your heat she gets huffy
Simply play on and 'Lay on, Macduffy!'
Brush up your Shakespeare
And they'll all kowtow.

Brush up your Shakespeare,
Start quoting him now,
Brush up your Shakespeare
And the women you will wow.
So tonight just recite to your matey
'Kiss me, Kate, Kiss me, Kate, Kiss me, Katey',
Brush up your Shakespeare
And they'll all kowtow.

WILLIAM PLOMER
1903–73

———— ∞∞∞ ————

Born William Charles Franklyn Plomer to British parents in Pietersburg, South Africa, in 1903. His first novel, *Turbott Wolfe*, was published in 1926, and he co-founded the magazine *Voorslag* (Whiplash) with Roy Campbell that same year. Laurens van der Post also worked with them on *Voorslag*.

Plomer taught for two years in Japan, before coming to England in 1929, befriending Leonard and Virginia Woolf and settling in Bloomsbury. In 1937 he became principal reader for the publishers Jonathan Cape. Plomer wrote poetry, novels, edited Kilvert's diaries and wrote librettos for several of Benjamin Britten's operas, including *Gloriana*, which Britten composed for the coronation of Elizabeth II in 1953. Plomer died in 1973.

75

FRENCH LISETTE: A BALLAD OF MAIDA VALE

Who strolls so late, for mugs a bait,
In the mists of Maida Vale,
Sauntering past a stucco gate
Fallen, but hardly frail?

You can safely bet that it's French Lisette,
The pearl of Portsdown Square,
On the game she has made her name
And rather more than her share.

In a coat of cony with her passport phony
She left her native haunts,
For an English surname exchanging *her* name
And then took up with a ponce.

Now a meaning look conceals the hook
Some innocent fish will swallow,
Chirping 'Hullo, Darling!' like a cheeky starling
She'll turn, and he will follow,

For her eyes are blue and her eyelids too
And her smile's by no means cryptic,
Her perm's as firm as if waved with glue,
She plies an orange lipstick,

And orange-red is her perky head
Under a hat like a tiny pie—
A pie on a tart, it might be said,
Is redundant, but oh, how spry!

From the distant tundra to snuggle under her
Chin a white fox was conveyed,
And with winks and leerings and Woolworth earrings
She's all set up for trade.

Now who comes here replete with beer?
A quinquagenarian clerk
Who in search of Life has left 'the wife'
And 'the kiddies' in Tufnell Park.

Dear sir, beware! for sex is a snare
And all is not true that allures.
Good sir, come off it! She means to profit
By this little weakness of yours:

Too late for alarm! Exotic charm
Has caught in his gills like a gaff,
He goes to his fate with a hypnotised gait,
The slave of her silvery laugh,

And follows her in to her suite of sin,
Her self-contained bower of bliss,
They enter her flat, she takes his hat,
And he hastens to take a kiss.

Ah, if only he knew that concealed from view
Behind a 'folk-weave' curtain
Is her fancy man, called Dublin Dan,
His manner would be less certain,

His bedroom eyes would express surprise,
His attitude less languor,
He would watch his money, not call her 'Honey',
And be seized with fear or anger.

Of the old technique one need scarcely speak,
But oh, in the quest for Romance
'Tis folly abounding in a strange surrounding
To be divorced from one's pants.

JOYCE GRENFELL
1910–79

⬣

Joyce Grenfell was born in London 1910. Her father, an architect, worked with Sir Edwin Lutyens, and she was the niece of Viscountess Astor, born in London in 1910. She made her stage debut in *The Little Revue* in 1939. Following a recommendation by Noël Coward she joined ENSA, entertaining the troops in such far-flung places as Baghdad, Jerusalem, Malta, Tunis, Algiers, Gibraltar, Tehran, Cairo, Bombay, Madras, Delhi, Calcutta and Damascus. She appeared in many one-woman shows of her comic monologues. She starred in the St Trinian films and wrote two volumes of autobiography, *Joyce Grenfell Requests the Pleasure* (1976) and *George, Don't Do That* (1977). She died in 1979, survived by her husband Reggie.

76

STATELY AS A GALLEON

My neighbour, Mrs Fanshaw, is portly-plump and gay,
She must be over sixty-seven, if she is a day.
You might have thought her life was dull,
It's one long whirl instead.
I asked her all about it, and this is what she said:

I've joined an Olde Thyme Dance Club, the trouble is
    that there
Are too many ladies over, and no gentlemen to spare.
It seems a shame, it's not the same,
But still it has to be,
Some ladies have to dance together,
One of them is me.

Stately as a galleon, I sail across the floor,
Doing the Military Two-step, as in the days of yore.
I dance with Mrs Tiverton; she's light on her feet, in
    spite
Of turning the scale at fourteen stone, and being of
    medium height.
So gay the band,
So giddy the sight,
Full evening dress is a must,
But the zest goes out of a beautiful waltz
When you dance it bust to bust.

Grenfell

So, stately as two galleons, we sail across the floor,
Doing the Valse Valeta as in the days of yore.
The gent is Mrs Tiverton, I am her lady fair,
She bows to me ever so nicely and I curtsey to her
   with care.
So gay the band,
So giddy the sight,
But it's not the same in the end
For a lady is never a gentleman, though
She may be your bosom friend.

So, stately as a galleon, I sail across the floor,
Doing the dear old Lancers, as in the days of yore.
I'm led by Mrs Tiverton, she swings me round and
   round
And though she manoeuvres me wonderfully well
I never get off the ground.
So gay the band,
So giddy the sight,
I try not to get depressed.
And it's done me a power of good to explode,
And get this lot off my chest.

SIR JOHN COLLINGS SQUIRE
1884–1958

———∞∞∞———

Sir John Squire was born in Plymouth in 1884 and educated at Blundell's School before going to St John's College, Cambridge. He later became Literary Editor of the *New Statesman* and his books of light verse included *Parnassus* and *Tricks of the Trade*.

77

IF GRAY HAD HAD TO WRITE HIS ELEGY IN THE CEMETERY OF
SPOON RIVER INSTEAD OF IN THAT OF STOKE POGES

The curfew tolls the knell of parting day,
　The whippoorwill salutes the rising moon,
And wanly glimmer in her gentle ray
　The sinuous windings of the turbid Spoon.

Here where the flattering and mendacious swarm
　Of lying epitaphs their secrets keep,
At last incapable of further harm,
　The lewd forefathers of the village sleep.

The earliest drug of half-awakened morn,
　Cocaine or hashish, strychnine, poppy-seeds
Or fiery produce of fermented corn
　No more shall start them on the day's misdeeds.

For them no more the whetstone's cheerful noise,
　No more the sun upon his daily course
Shall watch them savouring the genial joys
　Of murder, bigamy, arson and divorce.

Here they all lie; and, as the hour is late,
   O stranger, o'er their tombstones cease to stoop,
But bow thine ear to me and contemplate
   The unexpurgated annals of the group.

Here are two hundred only: yet of these
   Some thirty died of drowning in the river,
Sixteen went mad, ten others had DT"s,
   And twenty-eight cirrhosis of the liver.

Several by absent-minded friends were shot,
   Still more blew out their own exhausted brains,
One died of a mysterious inward rot,
   Three fell off roofs, and five were hit by trains.

One was harpooned, one gored by a bull-moose,
   Four on the Fourth fell victims to lock-jaw,
Ten in electric chair or hempen noose
   Suffered the last exaction of the law.

Stranger, you quail, and seem inclined to run;
But, timid stranger, do not be unnerved;
I can assure you that there was not one
   Who got a tithe of what he had deserved.

Full many a vice is born to thrive unseen,
   Full many a crime the world does not discuss,
Full many a pervert lives to reach a green
   Replete old age, and so it was with us.

Here lies a parson who would often make
  Clandestine rendezvous with Claflin's Moll,
And 'neath the druggist's counter creep to take
  A sip of surreptitious alcohol.

And here a doctor, who had seven wives,
  And, fearing this *ménage* might seem grotesque,
Persuaded six of them to spend their lives
  Locked in a drawer of his private desk.

And others here there sleep who, given scope,
  Had writ their names large on the Scrolls of Crime,
Men who, with half a chance, might haply cope
  With the first miscreants of recorded time.

Doubtless in this neglected spot was laid
  Some village Nero who had missed his due,
Some Bluebeard who dissected many a maid,
  And all for naught, since no one ever knew.

Some poor bucolic Borgia here may rest
  Whose poisons sent whole families to their doom.
Some hayseed Herod who, within his breast,
  Concealed the sites of many an infant's tomb.

Types that the Muse of Masefield might have stirred,
  Or waked to ecstasy Gaboriau,
Each in his narrow cell at last interred,
  All, all are sleeping peacefully below.

Enough, enough! But, stranger, ere we part,
   Glancing farewell to each nefarious bier,
This warning I would beg you to take to heart,
   'There is an end to even the worst career!'

ALAN BENNETT
born 1934

───────⊗⊗⊗───────

The son of a butcher, Bennett was born in Leeds in 1934 and educated at the Leeds Modern School and Exeter College, Oxford. Following his National Service he became a junior lecturer in Modern History at Magdalen College, Oxford, from 1960 to 1962. During this period he performed in the satirical revue *Beyond the Fringe* with Jonathan Miller, Peter Cook and Dudley Moore. His first stage play, *Forty Years On*, was produced in 1968, followed by *The Old Country*, *Single Spies*, *An Englishman Abroad* and *A Question of Attribution*.

He also adapted Kenneth Grahame's *Wind in the Willows* and wrote *The Madness of George III*, which was very succcessful both on stage and screen.

His autobiography, *Writing Home*, was published in 1994.

78

PLACE-NAMES OF CHINA

Bolding Vedas! Shanks New Nisa!
Trusty Lichfield swirls it down
To filter beds on Ruislip Marshes
From my lav in Kentish Town.

The Burlington! The Rochester!
Oh those names of childhood loos—
Nursie rattling at the door-knob:
'Have you done your Number Twos?'

Lady typist – office party—
Golly! All that gassy beer!
Tripping home down Hendon Parkway
To her Improved Windermere.

Here I sit, alone and sixty,
Bald and fat and full of sin,
Cold the seat and loud the cistern
As I read the Harpic tin.

W. H. AUDEN

(see page 139 for biography)

(see page 139 for biography)

79

DOGGEREL BY A SENIOR CITIZEN
for Robert Lederer

Our earth in 1969
Is not the planet I call mine,
The world, I mean, that gives me strength
To hold off chaos at arm's length.

My Eden landscapes and their climes
Are constructs from Edwardian times,
When bath-rooms took up lots of space,
And, before eating, one said Grace.

The automobile, the aeroplane,
Are useful gadgets, but profane:
The enginry of which I dream
Is moved by water or by steam.

Reason requires that I approve
The light-bulb which I cannot love:
To me more reverence-commanding
A fish-tail burner on the landing.

My family ghosts I fought and routed,
Their values, though, I never doubted:
I thought their Protestant Work-Ethic
Both practical and sympathetic.

When couples played or sang duets,
It was immoral to have debts:
I shall continue till I die
To pay in cash for what I buy.

The Book of Common Prayer we knew
Was that of 1662:
Though with-it sermons may be well,
Liturgical reforms are hell.

Sex was, of course – it always is—
The most enticing of mysteries,
But news-stands did not yet supply
Manichaean pornography.

Then Speech was mannerly, an Art,
Like learning not to belch or fart:
I cannot settle which is worse,
The Anti-Novel or Free Verse.

Nor are those PhD's my kith,
Who dig the symbol and the myth:
I count myself a man of letters
Who writes, or hopes to, for his betters.

Dare any call Permissiveness
An educational success?
Saner those class-rooms which I sat in,
Compelled to study Greek and Latin.

Though I suspect the term is crap,
If there *is* a Generation Gap,
Who is to blame? Those, old or young,
Who will not learn their Mother-Tongue.

But Love, at least, is not a state
Either *en vogue* or out-of-date,
And I've true friends, I will allow,
To talk and eat with here and now.

Me alienated? Bosh! It's just
As a sworn citizen who must
Skirmish with it that I feel
Most at home with what is Real.

Goodgers – Roger McGough

This is from his 1988 book of children's poems *Imaginary Menagerie*, a volume featuring animals of McGough's own creation, e.g. 'The Allivator', a cross between an elevator and an alligator. Lying in bed one morning, thinking about badgers (as one does), Roger reasoned that the opposite of bad being good, *ipso facto* the antonym to badger must be 'Goodger'.

80

GOODGERS

Once upon a time,
there lived in the forest
Badgers and Goodgers

Badgers emerged only after dark
using foul language,
and gobbled up all the blind dormice,
deaf bats and lame frogs
they could lay their greasy claws on,
as well as choice morsels of any child
who happened to wander innocently
into the forest, way past its bedtime.

Goodgers, on the other hand,
were bright-eyed and light as marshmallows.
They loved to dance in the sunshine
and could sing in many languages.
When not jogging or clearing litter
they nibbled moon beans and alfresco sprouts
and ate lots of fibre.

And then suddenly, without warning,
there came The Great Drought
followed by The Great Fire
followed by The Great Flood
followed by The Great Plague

followed by The Great Jazz Revival
And when finally The Great Famine
took the forest by the throat

It was the Badgers
who wheeled and dealed
and looted and hoarded.
Who connived, ducked and dived.

And it was the Goodgers
who cared and shared
and helped those
less fortunate than themselves.

Unfortunately,
the less fortunate survived
and the Goodgers perished.
Which just goes to show.

And so when Pan
(The Great Spirit of the Animal Kingdom)
returned to the forest after a fortnight in Portugal
he was saddened by the demise of the Goodgers
and determined that they should not be forgotten.

So, dipping a finger
into the pure white pool of Goodger memory,
he annointed the heads of the Badgers
who immediately gave up swearing and eating children.

And to this very day,
Badgers still wear the distinctive white mark
on their coats   (As far as I know.)

LOUIS MacNEICE
1907–63

———— ❦ ————

Born in Belfast in 1907, Frederick Louis MacNeice was the son of a rector who became the Bishop of Down and Connor and Dromore. Educated at Marlborough, where he, Betjeman and Anthony Blunt were school chums, he went up to Merton College, Oxford, having already published his first book of poems, *Blind Fireworks*. During the 1930s MacNeice lectured in classics in Birmingham and London, while being associated in poetry circles with Auden, Spender and Cecil Day-Lewis.

After lecturing in America during the first year of the Second World War, he returned to Britain, joining the Features Department at the BBC, where he remained as a writer and producer until 1961. After resigning, he continued as a freelance writer of poems, radio plays and stage plays.

He died in 1963 after catching a cold whilst visiting a mine.

81

BAGPIPE MUSIC

It's no go the merrygoround, it's no go the rickshaw,
All we want is a limousine and a ticket for the peepshow.
Their knickers are made of crêpe-de-chine, their shoes
   are made of python,
Their halls are lined with tiger rugs and their walls with
   heads of bison.

John MacDonald found a corpse, put it under the sofa,
Waited till it came to life and hit it with a poker,
Sold its eyes for souvenirs, sold its blood for whisky,
Kept its bones for dumb-bells to use when he was fifty.

It's no go the Yogi-Man, it's no go Blavatsky,
All we want is a bank balance and a bit of skirt in a
   taxi.

Annie MacDougall went to milk, caught her foot in the
   heather,
Woke to hear a dance record playing of Old Vienna.
It's no go your maidenheads, it's no go your culture,
All we want is a Dunlop tyre and the devil mend the
   puncture.

The Laird o' Phelps spent Hogmanay declaring he was
   sober,
Counted his feet to prove the fact and found he had one
   foot over.
Mrs Carmichael had her fifth, looked at the job with
   repulsion,
Said to the midwife 'Take it away; I'm through with
   over-production'.

It's no go the gossip column, it's no go the ceilidh,
All we want is a mother's help and a sugar-stick for
   the baby.

Willie Murray cut his thumb, couldn't count the damage,
Took the hide of an Ayrshire cow and used it for a
   bandage.
His brother caught three hundred cran when the seas
   were lavish,
Threw the bleeders back in the sea and went upon
   the parish.

It's no go the Herring Board, it's no go the Bible,
All we want is a packet of fags when our hands are
   idle.

It's no go the picture palace, it's no go the stadium,
It's no go the country cot with a pot of pink geraniums,
It's no go the Government grants, it's no go the elections,
Sit on your arse for fifty years and hang your hat on a
   pension.

It's no go my honey love, it's no go my poppet;
Work your hands from day to day, the winds will blow
  the profit.
The glass is falling hour by hour, the glass will fall
  for ever,
But if you break the bloody glass you won't hold up the
  weather.

E. V. KNOX

(see page 121 for biography)

82

THE DIRECTOR

They made me a director,
   I dreamt it in a dream;
I was a print collector
   And owned a salmon stream.

They made me a director
   Of companies one or two;
I did not fear the spectre
   Of Nemesis – would you?

They made me a director
   Of companies two or three;
I bought myself a sector
   Of Sussex, near the sea.

They made me a director
   Of companies three or four;
I had a man named Hector
   To answer the front-door.

They made me a director
  Of companies four or five;
The beams of my reflector
  Lit up the laurelled drive.

They made me a director
  Of companies five or six;
I was a stern protector
  Of meal-fed pheasant chicks.

They made me a director
  Of companies six or seven
No shareholding objector
  Opposed my path to heaven.

They made me a director
  Of companies seven or eight;
The income-tax collector
  Knelt down before my gate.

They made me a director
  Of companies eight or nine;
I drank the golden nectar
  And had no other wine.

They made me a director
  Of companies nine or ten—

'Hullo, police-inspector!
  Good morning, plain-clothes men!'

J. B. MORTON
1893–1979

Born in London in 1893, John Cameron Andrew Bingham Michael Morton was educated at a prep school in Kingston-upon-Thames, then Harrow and Oxford. He left university in 1912, declaring that he was going to be a poet. For the next two years he wrote for the Revue Theatre (his father was a librettist and adapted Lehan's *Merry Widow* into English).

In 1914 he joined the Royal Fusiliers as a private before getting a commission with the Suffolk Regiment. Following shell-shock on the Somme he worked for military intelligence. He published a novel, *The Barber of Putney*, in 1919, and the same year became a staff columnist on the *Sunday Express*, later transferring to the *Daily Express*. Morton inherited the humorous 'Beachcomber' column, following in the footsteps of Mason J. B. Arbuthnot, who wrote it as 'Sassenach', and D. B. Wyndham Lewis. In 1927 Morton married Mary O'Leary and moved to Worthing, Sussex, from where he sent in his daily 'Beachcomber' column. He continued to write 'Beachcomber' until late 1975.

83

MISTAKEN IDENTITY

The smiling film-star stood, to meet
The mob that surged along the street.
Before the man could say a word
They charged him like a maddened herd,
And knocked him down and trampled him,
And almost tore him limb from limb.
Then, laughing wildly through their tears,
They ripped his clothes for souvenirs,
Snatched bits of trouser, strips of shirt,
And left him lying in the dirt.
But one, whose wits were wide awake,
Knew they had made a slight mistake,
And thus addressed the hideous throng:
'Hi! Wait a bit! We've got it wrong!
Oh, damn it all! Take it from me,
He's not the one we came to see.'

EDWARD LEAR

(see page 4 for biography)

84

THE TWO OLD BACHELORS

Two old Bachelors were living in one house;
One caught a Muffin, the other caught a Mouse.
Said he who caught the Muffin to him who caught the
    Mouse,—
'This happens just in time! For we've nothing in the
    house,
'Save a tiny slice of lemon and a teaspoonful of honey,
'And what to do for dinner – since we haven't any
    money?
'And what can we expect if we haven't any dinner,
'But to lose our teeth and eyelashes and keep on growing
    thinner?'

Said he who caught the Mouse to him who caught the
    Muffin,—
'We might cook this little Mouse, if we only had some
    Stuffin'!
'If we had but Sage and Onion we could do extremely
    well,
'But how to get that Stuffin' it is difficult to tell'—

Those two old Bachelors ran quickly to the town
And asked for Sage and Onions as they wandered up
    and down;
They borrowed two large Onions, but no Sage was to
    be found
In the Shops, or in the Market, or in all the Gardens round.

But some one said, – 'A hill there is, a little to the north,
'And to its purpledicular top a narrow way leads forth;—
'And there among the rugged rocks abides an ancient
    Sage,—
'An earnest Man, who reads all day a most perplexing
    page.
'Climb up, and seize him by the toes! – all studious as
    he sits,—
'And pull him down, – and chop him into endless
    little bits!
'Then mix him with your Onion, (cut up likewise into
    Scraps,)—
'When your Stuffin' will be ready – and very good:
    perhaps.'

Those two old Bachelors without loss of time
The nearly purpledicular crags at once began to climb;
And at the top, among the rocks, all seated in a nook,
They saw that Sage, a reading of a most enormous
    book.

'You earnest Sage!' aloud they cried, 'your book you've
    read enough in!—
'We wish to chop you into bits to mix you into Stuffin'!'—

But that old Sage looked calmly up, and with his awful
  book,
At those two Bachelors' bald heads a certain aim he
  took;—
And over Crag and precipice they rolled promiscuous
  down,—
At once they rolled, and never stopped in lane or field
  or town,—
And when they reached their house, they found (besides
  their want of Stuffin',)
The Mouse had fled; – and, previously, had eaten up the
  Muffin.

They left their home in silence by the once convivial
  door.
And from that hour those Bachelors were never heard
  of more.

E. C. BENTLEY
1875–1956

———— ∞∞∞ ————

Edmund Clerihew Bentley was the son of a civil servant. He was called to the Bar, but made journalism his career. A life-long friend of G. K. Chesterton, Bentley initially achieved fame for his innovative detective novel, *Trent's Last Case*. He originated a kind of poem which he called 'A sort of formless four line verse', which became known as the Clerihew.

85

Sir Christopher Wren,
Said, 'I am going to dine with some men,
If anyone calls
Say I'm designing St Paul's.'

PAM AYRES

(see page 53 for biography)

86

THE DOLLY ON THE DUSTCART

I'm the dolly on the dustcart,
I can see you're not impressed,
I'm fixed above the driver's cab,
With wire across me chest,
The dustman see, he notice me,
Going in the grinder,
And he fixed me on the lorry,
I dunno if that was kinder.

This used to be a lovely dress,
In pink and pretty shades,
But it's torn now, being on the cart,
And black as the ace of spades,
There's dirt all round me face,
And all across me rosy cheeks,
Well, I've had me head thrown back,
But we ain't had no rain for weeks.

I used to be a 'Mama' doll,
Tipped forward, I'd say 'Mum';
But the rain's got in me squeaker,
And now I been struck dumb,

I had two lovely blue eyes,
But out in the wind and weather,
One's sunk back in me head like,
And one's gone altogether.

I'm not a soft, flesh-coloured dolly
Modern children like so much,
I'm one of those hard old dollies,
What are very cold to touch,
Modern dollies' underwear
Leaves me a bit nonplussed,
I haven't got a bra,
But then I haven't got a bust!

But I was happy in that dolls' house,
I was happy as a Queen,
I never knew that Tiny Tears
Was coming on the scene,
I heard of dolls with hair that grew,
And I was quite enthralled,
Until I realised *my* head
Was hard and pink . . . and bald.

So I travel with the rubbish,
Out of fashion, out of style,
Out of me environment,
For mile after mile,
No longer prized . . . dustbinised!
Unfeminine, untidy,
I'm the dolly on the dustcart.
And there's no collection Friday.

NIGEL FORDE

*(see page 167 for biography
and background to this poem)*

87

SEA FRET

I must down to the seas again,
To the lonely sea and the sky,
Where half a million shoulderblades
Are oiled and ready to fry;
And bodies that winter has gratefully veiled
Come out and appal the eye;

And father is bluff and hearty and scoffs:
'Just a crab! Pick it up! Be a man!'
And he picks it up with a chuckle of scorn
And loses the use of one hand;
And grandmother ponders the memories brought
By a gusset full of sand;

And the local youths have constructed a goal
Out of jackets and cans of beer;
'To me! Barry! To me! To me!
Barry! To me! Over here!'
And the girls, unimpressed go on building a nest
Of crash-helmets and Ambre-Solaire;

Forde

While the wholemeal parents have taken Cassandra
For an ecological spin
To the farming museum, the butterfly park
And the oak that cloaked a King,
When all she wants is a bucket and spade
And a friend with a cockney grin;

And Kevin, by accident, brushes the hand
Of his next-door neighbour's daughter
Who watches the tide receding as fast
As the things that her mother has taught her,
And the darkling beach spins a long double line
Of footprints filling with water;

And the boarding-house smell (of wet plimsolls and gas
And polish) pervades the gloom
Where father watches the Test highlights
In the bare little TV room;
And mother is hopeful in underwear
Like she wore on her honeymoon;

And when it's all over, the luggage is lugged,
And everyone's tired and snappy,
For they got up to pack at a quarter past five
And the baby's just filled his fourth nappy;
Was it worth all the bother? For only the dog
Has been *truly* and *blissfully* happy.

The Fat White Woman Speaks – G. K. Chesterton

This poem is the 'sometimes criticised – sometimes applauded' response of G. K. Chesterton to Frances Cornford's 'To a Fat Lady Seen From the Train', first published in her 1911 collection *Poems*.

Here is Cornford's original poem, and Chesterton's response.

FRANCES CORNFORD

TO A FAT LADY SEEN FROM THE TRAIN

O why do you walk through the fields in gloves,
   Missing so much and so much?
O fat white woman whom nobody loves,
Why do you walk through the fields in gloves,
When the grass is soft as the breast of doves
   And shivering-sweet to the touch?
O why do you walk through the fields in gloves,
   Missing so much and so much?

G. K. CHESTERTON

88

THE FAT WHITE WOMAN SPEAKS

Why do you rush through the field in trains,
Guessing so much and so much.
Why do you flash through the flowery meads,
Fat-head poet that nobody reads;
And why do you know such a frightful lot
About people in gloves as such?
And how the devil can you be sure,
Guessing so much and so much,
How do you know but what someone who loves
Always to see me in nice white gloves
At the end of the field you are rushing by,
Is waiting for his Old Dutch?

The Stately Homes of England – Noël Coward

'The Stately Homes of England' made its first appearance in *Operette*, which opened on 16 March 1938 at His Majesty's, London, after a try-out in Manchester, with book music and lyrics by Coward.

89

THE STATELY HOMES OF ENGLAND

Lord Elderley, Lord Borrowmere, Lord Sickert and Lord
  Camp,
With every virtue, every grace,
Ah! what avails the sceptred race.
Here you see the four of us,
And there are so many more of us,
Eldest sons that must succeed.
We know how Caesar conquered Gaul
And how to whack a cricket ball,
Apart from this our education
Lacks co-ordination.
Tho' we're young and tentative
And rather rip-representative
Scions of a noble breed,
We are the products of those homes serene and stately
Which only lately
Seem to have run to seed!

  The Stately Homes of England
  How beautiful they stand,
  To prove the upper classes
  Have still the upper hand;
  Tho' the fact that they have to be rebuilt
  And frequently mortgaged to the hilt
  Is inclined to take the gilt

Off the gingerbread,
And certainly damps the fun
Of the eldest son.
But still we won't be beaten,
We'll scrimp and screw and save,
The playing-fields of Eton
Have made us frightfully brave,
And tho' if the Van Dycks have to go
And we pawn the Bechstein Grand,
We'll stand by the Stately Homes of England.

Here you see the pick of us,
You may be heartily sick of us
Still with sense we're all imbued.
We waste no time on vain regrets
And when we're forced to pay our debts
We're always able to dispose of
Rows and rows and rows of
Gainsboroughs and Lawrences,
Some sporting prints of Aunt Florence's,
Some of which are rather rude.
Altho' we sometimes flaunt our family conventions,
Our good intentions
Mustn't be misconstrued.

The Stately Homes of England
We proudly represent,
We only keep them up for
Americans to rent.
Tho' the pipes that supply the bathroom burst

And the lavatory makes you fear the worst,
It was used by Charles the First
Quite informally,
And later by George the Fourth
On a journey North.
The State Apartments keep their
Historical renown,
It's wiser not to sleep there
In case they tumble down;
But still if they ever catch on fire
Which, with any luck, they might,
We'll fight for the Stately Homes of England.

The Stately Homes of England,
Tho' rather in the lurch,
Provide a lot of chances
For psychical research.
There's the ghost of a crazy younger son
Who murdered in Thirteen Fifty One
An extremely rowdy nun
Who resented it,
And people who come to call
Meet her in the hall.
The baby in the guest wing
Who crouches by the grate,
Was walled up in the west wing
In Fourteen Twenty Eight.
If anyone spots the Queen of Scots
In a hand-embroidered shroud,
We're proud of the Stately Homes of England.

VICTORIA WOOD
born 1953

———— ❤❤❤ ————

Born in Prestwich, Lancashire, Victoria Wood first became well-known because of her appearances on BBC TV's *That's Life*. In 1978 her television play *Talent* was a great success and won her the Pye Award for Most Promising New Writer. A comedienne who writes her own sketches, she also teamed up with Julie Walters in the early 1980s for the TV series *Wood and Walters*, and has had many other hit shows including *An Audience with Victoria Wood* and *Victoria Wood As Seen on TV*. She frequently tours her own stage shows, which have included sell-out appearances at London's Royal Albert Hall.

90

SATURDAY NIGHT

Oh dear what can the matter be?
Eight o'clock at night on a Saturday
Tracey Clegg and Nicola Battersby
Coming to town double quick.

They rendezvous in front of a pillar
Tracey's tall like Jonathan Miller
Nicola's more like Guy the Gorilla
If Guy the Gorilla were thick.

Their hair's been done it's very expensive
Their use of mousse and gel is extensive
As weapons their heads would be classed as offensive
And put under some kind of ban.

They're covered in perfumes but these are misnomers
Nicola's scent could send dogs into comas
Tracey's kills insects and dustbin aromas
And also gets stains off the pan.

> *Chorus:*
> But it's their night out
> It's what it's all about
> Looking for lads
> Looking for fun

Wood

A burger and chips with a sesame bun
They're in the mood
For a fabulous interlude
Of living it up
Painting the town
Drinking Bacardi and keeping it down
But it's all all right
It's what they do of a Saturday night.

Oh dear what can the matter be?
What can that terrible crunching and clatter be?
It's the cowboy boots of Nicola Battersby
Leading the way into town.

They hit the pub and Tracey's demeanour
Reminds you of a loopy hyena
They have sixteen gins and a rum and Ribena
And this is before they've sat down.

They dare a bloke from Surrey called Murray
To phone the police and order a curry
He gets locked up, it's a bit of a worry
But they won't have to see him again.

They're dressed to kill and looking fantastic
Tracey's gone for rubber and plastic
Nicola's dress is a piece of elastic
It's under a heck of a strain.

Chorus:
But it's their night out
It's what it's all about
Ordering drinks
Ordering cabs
Making rude gestures with doner kebabs
They're in the mood
For a fabulous interlude
Of weeing in parks
Treading on plants
Getting their dresses caught up in their pants
And it's all all right
It's what they do of a Saturday night.

Oh dear what can the matter be?
What can that terrible slurping and splatter be?
It's Tracey Clegg and Nicola Battersby
Snogging with Derek and Kurt.

They're well stuck in to heavyish petting
It's far too dark to see what you're getting
Tracey's bra flies off, how upsetting
And several people are hurt.

Oh dear, oh dear
Oh dear, oh dear

Wood

Oh dear what can the matter be?
What can that motheaten pile of old tatters be?
It's Tracey Clegg and Nicola Battersby
Getting chucked off the last Ninety-Two.

With miles to go and no chance of hitching
And Nicola's boots have bust at the stitching
Tracey laughs and says what's the point bitching
I couldn't give a bugger, could you?

91

IN DEFENCE OF HEDGEHOGS

I am very fond of hedgehogs
Which makes me want to say,
That I am struck with wonder,
How there's any left today,
For each morning as I travel
And no short distance that,
All I see are hedgehogs,
Squashed. And dead. And flat.

Now. Hedgehogs are not clever,
No, hedgehogs are quite dim,
And when he sees your headlamps,
Well, it don't occur to him,
That the very wisest thing to do
Is up and run away,
No! he curls up in a stupid ball,
And no doubt starts to pray.

Well, motor cars do travel
At a most alarming rate,
And by the time you sees him,
It is very much too late,

And thus he gets a-squasho'd,
Unrecorded but for me,
With me pen and paper,
Sittin' in a tree.

It is statistically proven,
In chapter and in verse,
That in a car and hedgehog fight,
The hedgehog comes off worse,
When whistlin' down your prop shaft,
And bouncin' off your diff,
His coat of nice brown prickles,
Is not effect-iff.

A hedgehog cannot make you laugh,
Whistle, dance or sing,
And he ain't much to look at,
And he don't make anything,
And in amongst his prickles,
There's fleas and bugs and that,
But there ain't no need to leave him,
Squashed. And dead. And flat.

Oh spare a thought for hedgehogs,
Spare a thought for me,
Spare a thought for hedgehogs,
As you drink your cup of tea,
Spare a thought for hedgehogs,
Hoverin' on the brinkt,
Spare a thought for hedgehogs,
Lest they become extinct.

JOHN BETJEMAN

(see page 45 for biography)

(see page 45 for biography)

$\boxed{92}$

EXECUTIVE

I am a young executive. No cuffs than mine are cleaner;
I have a Slimline brief-case and I use the firm's Cortina.
In every roadside hostelry from here to Burgess Hill
The *maîtres d'hôtel* all know me well and let me sign
   the bill.

You ask me what it is I do. Well actually, you know,
I'm partly a liaison man and partly PRO.
Essentially I integrate the current export drive
And basically I'm viable from ten o'clock till five.

For vital off-the-record work – that's talking
   transport-wise—
I've a scarlet Aston-Martin – and does she go? She flies!
Pedestrians and dogs and cats – we mark them down for
   slaughter.
I also own a speed-boat which has never touched the
   water.

She's built of fibre-glass, of course. I call her 'Mandy
  Jane'
After a bird I used to know – No soda, please, just
  plain—
And how did I acquire her? Well to tell you about that
And to put you in the picture I must wear my other hat.
I do some mild developing. The sort of place I need
Is a quiet country market town that's rather run to seed.
A luncheon and a drink or two, a little *savoir faire*—
I fix the Planning Officer, the Town Clerk and the Mayor.

And if some preservationist attempts to interfere
A 'dangerous structure' notice from the Borough Engineer
Will settle any buildings that are standing in our way—
The modern style, sir, with respect, has really come
  to stay.

$$\boxed{93}$$

BRIAN O LINN

Brian O Linn had no breeches to wear
He got an old sheepskin to make him a pair
With the fleshy side out and the woolly side in,
'They'll be pleasant and cool,' says Brian O Linn.

Brian O Linn had no shirt to his back,
He went to a neighbour's, and borrowed a sack,
Then he puckered the meal bag in under his chin—
'Sure they'll take them for ruffles,' says Brian O Linn.

Brian O Linn was hard up for a coat,
So he borrowed the skin of a neighbouring goat,
With the horns sticking out from his oxsters, and then,
'Sure they'll take them for pistols,' says Brian O Linn.

Brian O Linn had no hat to put on,
So he got an old beaver to make him a one,
There was none of the crown left and less of the brim,
'Sure there's fine ventilation,' says Brian O Linn.

Brian O Linn had no brogues for his toes,
He hopped in two crab-shells to serve him for those.
Then he split up two oysters that match'd like a twin,
'Sure they'll shine out like buckles,' says Brian O Linn.

Anonymous

Brian O Linn had no watch to put on,
So he scooped out a turnip to make him a one.
Then he placed a young cricket in – under the skin—
'Sure they'll think it is ticking,' says Brian O Linn.

Brian O Linn to his house had no door,
He'd the sky for a roof, and the bog for a floor;
He'd a way to jump out, and a way to swim in,
''Tis a fine habitation,' says Brian O Linn.

Brian O Linn went a-courting one night,
He set both the mother and daughter to fight;
To fight for his hand they both stripped to the skin,
'Sure! I'll marry you both,' says Brian O Linn.

Brian O Linn, his wife and wife's mother,
They all lay down in the bed together,
The sheets they were old and the blankets were thin,
'Lie close to the wall,' says Brian O Linn.

Brian O Linn, his wife and wife's mother,
Were all going home o'er the bridge together,
The bridge it broke down, and they all tumbled in,
'We'll go home by the water,' says Brian O Linn.

BRIAN PATTEN
born 1946

———— ⚮ ————

Born in Liverpool in 1946, Patten was educated at Sefton Park Secondary School, which he left at the age of fourteen. His working life began as a junior reporter on a local newspaper. At the same time he was publishing his own magazine, *Underdog*, featuring poems by local underground poets like Roger McGough and Adrian Henri. Patten, Henri and McGough gradually became known as 'the Liverpool poets'. Patten has been prolific throughout the 1960s, '70s, '80s and '90s, writing poetry, books for children and plays as well as frequently acting as a book editor.

94

SOMEWHERE BETWEEN HEAVEN AND WOOLWORTHS, A SONG

She keeps kingfishers in their cages
And goldfish in their bowls,
She is lovely and is afraid
Of such things as growing cold.

She's had enough men to please her,
Though they were more cruel than kind
And their love an act in isolation,
A form of pantomime.

She says she has forgotten
The feelings that she shared
At various all-night parties
Among the couples on the stairs,

For among the songs and dancing
She was once open wide,
A girl dressed in denim
With the boys dressed in lies.

She's eating roses on toast with tulip butter;
Praying for her mirror to stay young;
Though on its no longer gilted surface
This message she has scrawled:

'O somewhere between Heaven and Woolworths
I live I love I scold,
I keep kingfishers in their cages
And goldfish in their bowls.'

Poem With a Limp – Roger McGough

From his 1986 volume of poetry *Melting into the Foreground*, 'Poem with a Limp' was written in Portobello Road, Notting Hill Gate, the poet's home at the time. On climbing out of bed he was concerned to discover that he was walking with a limp. The panic, and the temporary impediment, had worn off by the time 'Poem with a Limp' was completed.

95

POEM WITH A LIMP

Woke up this morning with a
                                    limp.
Was it from playing
                        football
In my dreams? Arthrite's first
                                    arrow?
Polio? Muscular dystrophy? (A bit of
                                        each?)
I staggered around the kitchen spilling
                                            coffee
Before hobbling to the bank for
                                    lire
For the holiday I knew I would not be
                                        taking.
(For Portofino read Stoke
                            Mandeville.)
Confined to a wheelchair for the
                                    remainder
Of my short and tragic life.
                                Wheeled
On stage to read my terse, honest
                                    poems
Without a trace of bitterness. 'How
                                        brave,

And smiling still, despite the
                                    pain.'
Resigned now to a life of quiet
                                        fortitude
I plan the nurses' audition.
                                    Mid-afternoon
Sees me in the garden, sunning my
                                        limp.

It feels a little easier now.
Perhaps a miracle is on its way?
(Lourdes, W<small>II</small>.)

By opening-time the cure is complete.
I rise from my deck-chair:
'Look, everybody, I can walk, I can walk.'

WALTER DE LA MARE
1873–1956

———— ❦ ————

Born in Charlton, Kent, in 1873, Walter de la Mare was the son of a Bank of England official and related through his mother to Robert Browning. Educated at St Paul's Cathedral Choir School, where he founded the *Choristers' Journal*, he worked for twenty years for the Standard Oil Company as a clerk until Sir Henry Newbolt used his influence to secure de la Mare a Civil List pension of £100 a year.

He soon built up a formidable reputation, writing for both adults and children in his unique style. In company with Rupert Brooke and Wilfrid Gibson he contributed to the first volume of *Georgian Poetry*. As a beneficiary of Brooke's Will he was able to concentrate on his literary career, returning the favour by writing a critical study of Brooke as well as similar works on Lewis Carroll and Christina Rossetti. He was created a Companion of Honour and then awarded the Order of Merit in 1953. He died on 22 June 1956.

96

POOH!

Dainty Miss Apathy
Sat on a sofa,
Dangling her legs,
And with nothing to do;
She looked at a drawing of
Old Queen Victoria,
At a rug from far Persia—
An exquisite blue;
At a bowl of bright tulips;
A needlework picture
Of doves caged in wicker
You could almost hear coo;
She looked at the switch
That evokes e-
Lectricity;
At the coals of an age
BC millions and two—
When the trees were like ferns
And the reptiles all flew;
She looked at the cat
Asleep on the hearthrug,
At the sky at the window,—
The clouds in it, too;
And a marvellous light
From the West burning through:

And the one silly word
In her desolate noddle
As she dangled her legs,
Having nothing to do,
Was not, as you'd guess,
Of dumfoundered felicity,
But contained just four letters,
And these pronounced *POOH*!

PATRICK BARRINGTON
1908–1990

———— ❦ ————

Two of Barrington's best known poems, 'I Had A Duck-Billed Platypus' and 'Take Me In Your Arms, Miss Money-Penny Wilson' come from his book *Songs of a Sub-Man*.

97

TAKE ME IN YOUR ARMS, MISS MONEYPENNY-WILSON

Take me in your arms, Miss Moneypenny-Wilson,
   Take me in your arms, Miss Bates;
Fatal are your charms, Miss Moneypenny-Wilson,
   Fatal are your charms, Miss Bates;
Say you are my own, Miss Moneypenny-Wilson,
   Say you are my own, Miss Bates;
You I love alone, Miss Moneypenny-Wilson,
   You, and you alone, Miss Bates.

Sweet is the morn, Miss Moneypenny-Wilson;
   Sweet is the dawn, Miss B.,
But sweeter than the dawn and the daisies on the lawn
   Are you; sweet nymphs, to me.
Sweet, sweet, sweet is the sugar to the beet,
   Sweet is the honey to the bee,
But sweeter far than such sweets are
   Are your sweet names to me.

Deaf to my cries, Miss Moneypenny-Wilson,
   Deaf to my sighs, Miss B.,
Deaf to my songs and the story of my wrongs,
   Deaf to my minstrelsy;
Deafer than the newt to the sound of a flute,
   Deafer than a stone to the sea;
Deafer than a heifer to the sighing of a zephyr
   Are your deaf ears to me.

Cold, cold, cold as the melancholy mould,
   Cold as the foam-cold sea,
Colder than the shoulder of a neolithic boulder
   Are the shoulders you show to me.
Cruel, cruel, cruel is the flame to the fuel,
   Cruel is the axe to the tree,
But crueller and keener than a coster's concertina
   Is your cruel, cruel scorn to me.

RUPERT BROOKE
1887–1915

Rupert Brooke was born on 3 August 1887, the son of a Rugby schoolmaster. His interest in poetry was fired by reading Browning, and at Rugby he won poetry prizes as well as playing cricket and rugby. At King's College, Cambridge, he threw himself into university activities, immersing himself in the Drama and the Fabian Society, debating at the Union and becoming a member of the elite group known as the Apostles. It was at this period that he moved to his beloved Grantchester, just outside Cambridge, but an unhappy love affair in addition to other pressures culminated in a nervous breakdown.

The guiding hand of his main literary mentor Edward Marsh and his relationship with the actress Cathleen Nesbitt aided his recovery but he decided to clear his head through travel – to Canada, America and the South Sea Islands. After the outbreak of the First World War he joined the newly formed Royal Naval Division, and saw action in Antwerp before dying of septicaemia on 23 April 1915 en route to Gallipoli. Brooke was buried on the island of Skyros in the Aegean.

Sonnet: In Time of Revolt – Rupert Brooke

This was written in January 1908 when Brooke had just returned to King's College, Cambridge to sit exams, following a skiing trip to Andermatt, Switzerland. He had been to see *Peter Pan* and had just finished reading E. M. Forster's *The Celestial Omnibus*, so something in his hectic lifestyle had suggested 'Sonnet: In time of Revolt'. The poem was first published in the *Cambridge Review* on 6 February 1908; a fair copy in ink was mounted in a folio volume and donated by Edward Marsh in 1931 to the archive of King's College, Cambridge.

98

SONNET: IN TIME OF REVOLT

The thing must End. I am no boy! I AM
  NO BOY!! being twenty-one. Uncle, you make
  A great mistake, a very great mistake,
In childing me for letting slip a 'Damn!'
What's more, you called me 'Mother's one ewe lamb,'
  Bade me 'refrain from swearing – for *her* sake—
Till I'm grown up' . . . – By God! I think you take
Too much upon you, Uncle William!

You say I am your brother's only son
I know it. And, 'What of it?' I reply.
My heart's resolvèd. *Something must be done.*
So shall I curb, so baffle, so suppress
This too avuncular officiousness,
Intolerable consanguinuity

SYDNEY SMITH
1771–1845

After completing his education at Winchester and New College, Oxford, Smith went to Edinburgh as a tutor. There he helped found the influential journal *The Edinburgh Review*, before coming to London in 1803, where he lectured on moral philosophy and was involved in politics. He became a clergyman, living in Yorkshire and Somerset, before he was made a canon of St Paul's Cathedral in 1831.

Sydney Smith was famous as a wonderfully witty conversationalist and this humour shines through his writing as well.

89

RECIPE FOR A SALAD

To make this condiment, your poet begs
The pounded yellow of two hard-boiled eggs;
Two boiled potatoes, passed through kitchen-sieve,
Smoothness and softness to the salad give;
Let onion atoms lurk within the bowl,
And, half-suspected, animate the whole.
Of mordant mustard add a single spoon,
Distrust the condiment that bites so soon;
But deem it not, thou man of herbs, a fault,
To add a double quantity of salt.
And, lastly, o'er the flavored compound toss
A magic soup-spoon of anchovy sauce.
Oh, green and glorious! Oh, herbaceous treat!
'T would tempt the dying anchorite to eat;
Back to the world he'd turn his fleeting soul,
And plunge his fingers in the salad bowl!
Serenely full, the epicure would say,
Fate can not harm me, I have dined to-day!

WALTER SAVAGE LANDOR
1775–1864

———— ∞∞∞ ————

Born in 1775, Landor was educated at Rugby and Trinity College, Oxford, at least until he was sent down. In his youth he fought as a volunteer in Spain against the French, and was renowned for his violent temper. In 1795, aged twenty, he published some of his verse in *Poems*, followed three years later with an epic poem in seven books, *Gebir*.

He continued to publish poetry, and wrote a stage play that was never produced. In 1811 he married Julia Thullier, and the couple moved to Italy four years later, where they stayed until their separation in 1835. His output was prolific and Browning was a big fan of his work, but it seems his works haven't travelled well. Maybe their time will come again. Landor was the model for Lawrence Boythorn a character in Dickens's novel *Bleak House*. He died in 1864.

100

THE GEORGES

George the First was always reckoned
Vile, but viler George the Second;
And what mortal ever heard
Any good of George the Third?
When from earth the Fourth descended
(God be praised) the Georges ended.

Acknowledgements

John Murray (Publishers) Ltd for *Diary of a Church Mouse, How to get on in Society, Hunter Trials, A Subaltern's Love Song, Blame the Vicar, Christmas, Pot Pourri from a Surrey garden* and *Executive* by John Betjeman from his *Collected Poems*.

The Peters Fraser and Dunlop Group Limited on behalf of: The Estate of Hilaire Belloc © as printed in the original volume for *Matilda, The Hippopotamus, Henry King who chewed bits of string . . . , Rebecca, Jim* and *Lines to a Don*.

Papermac for *The Ruined Maid* from *The Complete Poems* by Thomas Hardy.

Faber & Faber Ltd for *Macavity: The Mystery Cat* and *Skimbleshanks: The Railway Cat* from *Old Possum's Book of Practical Cats* by T. S. Eliot.

A. P. Watt Ltd on behalf of The Royal Literary Fund for *The Rolling English Road, The Song against Grocers* and *The Fat White Woman Speaks* from *Answers To The Poets* by G. K. Chesterton.

John Johnson for *Warning* by Jenny Joseph.

Sheil Land Associates Ltd for *I wish I'd looked after me teeth, Dolly on the Dustcart* and *In Defence of Hedgehogs* from *The Works* by Pam Ayres published by BBC Books. © Pam Ayres 1992.

Curtis Brown London for *The Song of Mr Toad* and *Ducks' Ditty* from *The Wind In The Willows* by Kenneth Grahame copyright The University Chest, Oxford.

Andre Deutsch Ltd for *Tale of Custard The Dragon, England Expects* and *Curl Up And Diet* from *Candy is Dandy* by Ogden Nash.

The King's Breakfast taken from WHEN WE WERE VERY YOUNG by A. A. Milne, reprinted by permission of Methuen's Children's Books (a division of Egmont Children's Books).

Penguin UK for *Please Mrs Butler* by Allan Ahlberg (Kestrel Books 1983) Copyright © Allan Ahlberg 1983.

Professor Maria Fitzgerald for *The Everlasting Percy* and *The Director* by E. V. Knox.

David Higham Associates for *Betjeman 1984* by Charles Causley from his *Collected Poems*, published by Macmillan.

Faber and Faber Ltd for *The Unknown Citizen* and *Doggerel by a Senior Citizen* by W. H. Auden from his *Collected Poems*.

Acknowledgements

The Peters Fraser and Dunlop Group Limited on behalf of: Roger McGough © as printed in the original volume for *At Lunchtime*, *My Busseductress*, *Goodgers* and *Poem with a Limp*.

Robson Books for *A Day To Remember*, *Village Cricket* and *Sea Fret* by Nigel Forde.

Robson Books for *Popular Mythologies* by Vernon Scannell.

Faber and Faber Ltd for *Lonely Hearts* by Wendy Cope.

The Peters Fraser and Dunlop Group Limited on behalf of: Clive James © as printed in the original volume for *The Book Of My Enemy Has Been Remaindered*.

New Ground from Hugo Williams' *Selected Poems* (1989) by permission of Oxford University Press.

Rogers, Coleridge & White Ltd for *Love is . .* by Adrian Henri.

A. P. Watt Ltd on behalf of The Trustees of the Wodehouse Estate for *Printer's Error* by P. G. Wodehouse.

Private Eye for poem by E. J. Thribb.

Barry Humphries for *Megastar's Mantra*.

Random House UK for *French Lisette: A Ballad of Maida Vale* from *Collected Poems* by William Plomer published by Jonathan Cape.

Sheil Land Associates Ltd for *Stately As A Galleon* from *Stately As A Galleon* by Joyce Grenfell, published by Macmillan. Copyright © Joyce Grenfell 1978.

Papermac for *If Gray had had to write his Elegy* by Sir John Squires.

Place-names of China reprinted by permission of the Peters Fraser and Dunlop Group Ltd on behalf of: Alan Bennett © Forelake Ltd.

David Higham Associates for *Bagpipe Music* by Louis MacNeice from his *Collected Poems*, published by Faber and Faber.

The Peters Fraser and Dunlop Group Limited on behalf of: The Estate of J. B. Morton © as printed in the original volume for *Mistaken Identity*.

The Literary Trustees of Walter de la Mare and the Society of Authors as their representative for *Pooh!* by Walter de la Mare.

Faber and Faber Ltd for *Annus Mirabilis* by Philip Larkin from his *Collected Poems*.

Campbell Thomson and McLaughlin Limited for *What For* by Noel Petty from the anthology *This Poem Doesn't Rhyme*, edited by Gerard Benson and published by Puffin Books. © Noel Petty 1990.

INDEX OF POEM TITLES

336

INDEX OF FIRST LINES

338

Index of first lines